"You sure are a pretty little thing, Anna. Your mama will have to chase the boys off with a stick."

Anna's expression crinkled into a beaming toothless smile, and Justin chuckled.

An ache yawned in Meredith's chest, a sad yearning for the father she hadn't thought important only a year ago. She'd planned this baby, known she was going to raise her alone and had been prepared to be the only parent her child needed.

But that had been before. Before she'd seen Justin with his children…and with Anna in his arms.

"What's a frown doing on that pretty face?" Justin asked as he reached out and touched her between her brows. Her skin warmed like a schoolgirl's.

Meredith looked into his face, a face so darkly handsome and intriguingly expressive, and admitted a monumental truth to herself: she was attracted to this man. It was strong and exhilarating. And physical.

She was completely out of her comfort zone.

It felt…incredible.

CHERYL ST.JOHN

admits to being an avid collector who collects everything from blue and white transferware, teacups and paperweights to dolls, vintage fabrics and oil lamps. Her latest obsessions are ceramic pitchers and teapots. When not writing or enjoying her family, she can be found browsing antique malls and flea markets with her husband.

She says that knowing her stories bring hope and pleasure to readers is one of the best parts of being a writer. Cheryl was delighted to be asked to participate in the new LOGAN'S LEGACY series and especially appreciated exploring the edgy, yet sensitive subject matter in this story. She enjoyed the challenge and hopes her efforts bring you much reading pleasure.

Cheryl loves to hear from readers and you can write to her at: P.O. Box 24732, Omaha, NE 68124 or CherylStJ@aol.com.

LOGAN'S LEGACY
CHILD OF HER HEART
CHERYL ST.JOHN

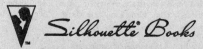
Silhouette Books

Published by Silhouette Books
America's Publisher of Contemporary Romance

Special thanks and acknowledgment are given
to Cheryl St.John for her contribution
to the LOGAN'S LEGACY series.

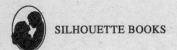 **SILHOUETTE BOOKS**

ISBN 0-373-61390-3

CHILD OF HER HEART

Visit Silhouette Books at www.eHarlequin.com

Printed in U.S.A.

Be a part of

ℒOGAN'S ℒEGACY

*Because birthright has its privileges
and family ties run deep.*

**After a sperm-bank mix-up, single mom
Meredith Malone got the shock of a lifetime....**

Meredith Malone: She survived breast cancer
and a fiancé's desertion. Now the birth of her
baby caused a scandal in the community. Meredith
had to protect her child, so she fled to a vacation
spot...and fell in love. Could she learn to trust again?

Justin Weber: A hotshot attorney determined
to protect the Children's Connection, Justin wanted
to learn more about Meredith and her baby. As he
spent time with her, he began to see his future in her
eyes....

Nurse Nancy Allen: A devoted health-care
worker, Nurse Nancy went to the authorities with
suspicions about a baby ring operating out of the
clinic. Could her speaking out have been a fatal
mistake?

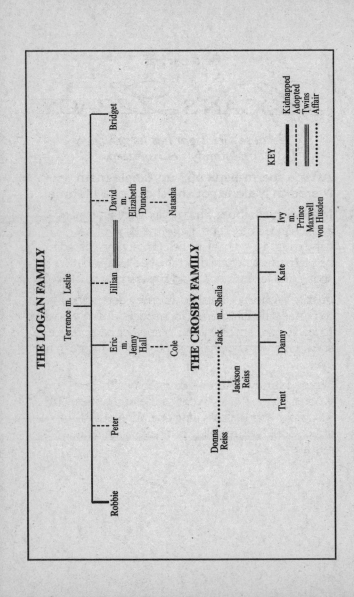

THE LOGAN FAMILY

Terrence m. Leslie

Robbie — Peter — Eric — Jillian ≡ David — Bridget
                     m.   m.
                     Jenny   Elizabeth
                     Hall   Duncan

Cole   Natasha

THE CROSBY FAMILY

Donna ·········· Jack ···· m. Sheila
Reiss

Jackson
Reiss

Trent — Danny — Kate — Ivy
                              m.
                              Prince
                              Maxwell
                              von Husden

KEY

Kidnapped
Adopted
Twins
Affair

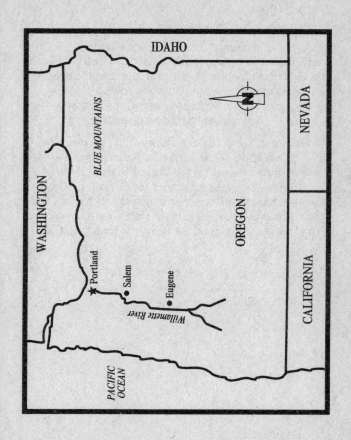

Special thanks to the following for their assistance
with factual details: RaeAnne Thayne
who shared her timely family vacation to Cannon Beach
in vivid detail; Bonnie Blythe who described the beaches
and recommended informational links; and to the
Johns Hopkins Breast Cancer Center experts
for answering medical questions.

Thanks to Susan Mallery, Pamela Toth, Laurie Paige,
Victoria Pade, Marie Ferrarella, Karen Rose Smith,
RaeAnne Thayne, Gina Wilkins, Elizabeth Bevarly,
Christie Ridgway and Anne Marie Winston, who
worked hard to pull together the continuity threads and
strengthen the series, and to Allison Lyons who quickly
and patiently answered questions and found solutions.

Prologue

"If the press gets wind of the mistake, the clinic's reputation is shot." Standing, Oliver Pearson leaned forward, one age-speckled hand on the polished mahogany table, and addressed the board of directors in his resonating deep voice. "I say we make a decision today. That baby was born nearly three months ago, and out of fear we've tabled the discussion long enough."

Dianna March straightened her already rigid spine in her leather chair, the overhead fluorescents highlighting her elegant silver pageboy. "We had to give the woman some time, Oliver, for goodness' sake! She gave birth to an African-American infant when she was expecting a child who looks like herself.

How insensitive would we look if we rushed right into her hospital room and asked her to sign waivers of release?"

Albert Squires, a balding, paunchy, retired executive, joined the discussion. "Miss Malone has had time. Her lawyer is calling and threatening to sue. The Children's Connection needs to offer compensation."

It was a generous offer coming from a man who'd worn the same burgundy suit to board meetings since 1995.

"A payoff is an admission of wrongdoing," Miles Remington, the youngest member of the board, disagreed. "Are we admitting responsibility?"

"The clinic *is* responsible," Dianna replied. "Someone mixed up the sperm from the donors and fertilized her eggs with sperm from an African-American."

"How do we know for certain that Miss Malone intends to sue?" John G. Reynolds asked, joining the conversation for the first time.

"Her mother's lawyer is asking for compensation," Oliver replied.

"The mother can't sue without the daughter," the man replied. "Perhaps this is a lot of blustering to see how much they can bleed us for without going public."

Terrence Logan, retired CEO of Logan Corporation, stood and walked to a table laden with a silver coffee urn and assorted pastries. He poured himself a steaming cup and returned to again fold his six-foot frame into his chair. "We've kept tabs through her doctor and her counselor at the clinic. What we need is someone to talk to the woman directly. Check her out, see where she stands on the issues and discover whether or not she's amenable to compensation."

"Justin's the man." Miles emphasized his words by jabbing his doughnut in the air. "Why isn't he here, anyway?"

Miles was referring to Justin Weber, the Logans' close family friend and corporate attorney for Children's Connection, one of the premier fertility clinics in the country.

"He's flying back from Chicago this afternoon," Terrence replied. "Late yesterday he settled with the insurance company over that fire incident."

"Send him to evaluate the Malone woman," Garnet Kearn said. She was a small woman with thin, wispy hair dyed a mousy brown and badly permed, making her head look like a large coconut. "That's his job."

"I don't think that's wise," Terrence said. "He's scheduled for his vacation, and I can't ask him to postpone it again. He's promised to take his boys to Cannon Beach."

He was referring to the company-owned suites in an elegant inn on the coast of Oregon where their executives, board members and corporate attorney shared privileges.

"When does he leave?" Albert asked.

Terrence took a sip of coffee. "He should have returned this morning, but he stayed over to wind up this Chicago deal."

Silence fell over the room. The clock on the wall ticked off the minutes like a time bomb.

Wayne Thorpe sat forward, his chair complaining beneath his considerable weight. The other board members looked to him with interest. He didn't speak often, but when he did, his words were usually worthy of listening. His nose and cheeks were florid from his nightly appointment with a bourbon bottle, and he wore heavy gold signet rings on both pinkies. "Things are probably tense for Meredith Malone," he said. "We need to consider her feelings in the matter. The board might be wise to give her more time to think over her situation and her choices."

No one said a word, digesting the suggestion, wondering where he was taking it.

Dianna March nodded her agreement.

"I'm sure there's an available suite at the Lighthouse Inn," Thorpe added. "It's February, after all, off-season."

Terrence looked decidedly uncomfortable.

Dianna's eyebrows rose.

As the implication sunk in, Thorpe's proposal was met with nods and sidelong glances. Send Meredith Malone to the same inn where their attorney would be vacationing.

"It would keep her away from the media awhile longer," Albert agreed.

"And give her some private time with her baby," Garnet said. "The clinic is all about families."

Terrence shook his head, but every person in the room, including him, knew something had to be done.

"Who will make the offer?" Miles asked.

"The chairman?" Wayne Thorpe suggested.

"Excellent idea." Oliver slapped the table as if banging a gavel. Murmurs of agreement echoed.

Dianna March was the chairwoman this term. Fitting that a woman should make the offer. As she tucked her hair behind one ear, diamonds glittered on her slender hand. "I'll see to it this afternoon."

One

Leaving Portland, Meredith Malone drove west along the Sunset Highway. Sweeping wheat fields bordered by verdant hills and towering mountains soon gave way to orchards, which gave way to forests of spruce, alder, cedar and hemlock. In places the highway cut in so deeply that the bases of the huge trees were eye level on both sides of the car, giving the feeling that she was an infinitesimal part of the endless forest. She drove in the shaded wilderness for an hour before seeing sunlight and sky again.

Here, an occasional gift shop dotted the sides of the road, joined by deserted fruit stands that would be busy in later months. During the summer even antique dealers displayed goods along this stretch of road, and tourists with RVs, towing ATVs or with bike and surfboard carriers slowed traffic considerably. This time of year, however, hers was one of only a few cars, so she made good time.

She descended the last hill from Saddle Mountain, pleased that she'd planned the drive for after her three-month-old daughter had been fed and was ready to sleep most of the morning.

She drove through a small river valley and climbed through the dense foliage along the coast. She hadn't been to the coast for years, and as she started the last descent toward Cannon Beach junction, the Pacific Ocean appeared, vast and surprisingly familiar. Ahead was a fleeting distant view of Haystack Rock, projecting a couple of hundred feet out of the water. From almost untouched countryside, she drove the steep loop down to Cannon Beach and into the small town.

From her car seat in the rear, Anna woke and let Meredith know she was hungry with tiny rooting sounds and a long wail of complaint.

"We're there, sweetie. Mommy just has to find the address."

She glanced at the piece of paper on the seat beside her and followed directions through the quaint little community to a multicolored brick inn near the beach. White shutters made the windows look welcoming, and each guest suite sported a sunny balcony. Shrubs bordered the building and lined the drive and the walk.

Meredith unfastened the carrier, grabbed Anna's bag and her purse, and carried the seat holding her baby. She would come back later for the rest of her belongings. Traveling with an infant was an enormous task. She had packed diapers and clothing and blankets and toys, and still she'd wondered if she'd remembered everything she would need for her stay. Once again she said a prayer of thanks for the blessing and ability to breast-feed. At least she didn't have to worry about bottles and formula.

It may have been a perfectly natural thing to a million women, but for her it was a gift she never took for granted.

Anna was red-faced and wailing by the time Meredith entered the lobby, set the carrier on the carpeted floor and checked in.

"Sorry," she said above the crying to the woman at the counter. "She's hungry."

The woman nodded. "Can I help you carry your things to your room? Maybe she'll settle down if you take her out and hold her."

"You're probably right." Meredith leaned over, unbuckled Anna's restraints and picked her up. Anna immediately quieted as she peered at her new surroundings and blinked at her mother.

"You've been cooped up in that seat for a while,

haven't you, sweetie?" Meredith smiled and turned back for the room key.

The clerk was staring at Anna.

Pain stabbed in Meredith's chest. Anna was a beautiful child with black hair, near-black eyes and velvety skin the color of coffee with cream. Meredith, on the other hand, was as fair-skinned as could be.

Would she ever get used to people staring at the two of them? She waited for a question—people often blurted the first thing on their minds. But this woman displayed a modicum of tact and said nothing.

With a cheerful smile pasted on her face, she came around the wall from the little room she'd been standing in and picked up the carrier and Meredith's bag. "I'll show you to your room."

Not "what a pretty baby" or "what is her name?" Meredith tamped down the hurt as the woman walked her down a hallway and led her to a set of double doors. Meredith used the plastic key card and let herself in. The hotel employee set her belongings just inside. "Have a nice stay."

"Thank you." Meredith closed the door and locked it. Her first impression was that the suite was as large as her apartment at home, but far more elegantly furnished.

Anna was fussing again, so without taking time to investigate the rooms, she hurried into the bedroom, placed the baby on the king-sized bed and changed her diaper. Then Meredith unbuttoned her shirt, settled in a comfortable overstuffed chair and placed Anna at her breast.

Dark eyes looked at her trustingly, smooth dark skin and lips a vivid contrast against Meredith's scarred white breast. She touched her baby's face and smiled. The drive had been beautiful and relaxing, but she was tired from packing and planning and following directions. She kicked off her shoes and propped her feet on a matching ottoman.

The past few months had been tension-filled and emotionally draining. No, the past couple of *years* had been tension-filled and emotionally draining. But the recent months had been worse, rife with her mother's constant disapproval and pressuring. Every time Meredith thought about her mother's reactions, renewed hurt knifed through her heart. Breathing deeply, she worked to fight back her anger before her tension seeped through to the baby in her arms.

Meredith's mother had wanted her to give up Anna for adoption. Meredith wouldn't hear of it. She'd loved her baby from conception. She'd adored her on sight and cherished her more every day since.

But Veronica was embarrassed. She'd been mortified when her daughter gave birth to an African-American child. She wanted the world to know Anna's birth was not by choice or by natural means and she threatened at every opportunity to feed the information about the mistake made by Children's Connection to the media in hopes of having the public's sympathy.

Veronica's obvious shame hurt Meredith more than she could say. She'd been surprised when she'd seen her baby, yes, of course. But ashamed? Certainly not. She was tired of fighting her mother on every front and constantly heading off her confrontations and insistence that Meredith sue Children's Connection. This was her *mother!* She should accept Meredith's decisions and *love* her grandchild.

Tears stung her eyelids and she determinedly blinked them away. She needed this time away from everything—especially from Veronica. She craved privacy. She was looking forward to peace and quiet, time alone with Anna without pressure or censure.

For a few blessed weeks, she wouldn't have to cook or clean; she'd have attendants to help tote and carry. She could see the local sights at her leisure and return here whenever she wanted to put her feet up and do nothing.

She glanced around the elegantly appointed room. This was just the getaway she needed.

Two

The morning news had predicted temperatures in the sixties and Meredith was glad for the unusual warmth. Shortly after her arrival the day before she had discovered a place nearby to rent all types of beach equipment, and she was eager to try out her canvas chair and umbrella.

The sand was deliciously warm from the sun, and though she knew the water was freezing cold, a few die-hard surfers in wet suits rode the waves onto the beach.

Anna slept peacefully on a thick blanket under the umbrella, and by late morning Meredith was a third of the way through a mystery novel she'd been wanting to read. She poured herself hot decaf coffee from the thermos, sipped leisurely and her eyes grew heavy.

"I think her baby's sleeping."

"She's sleeping, too, Lamond. Don't bother them."

"I'm not bothering them, I'm just lookin'."

The soft voices brought her out of her restful state, and she opened her eyes to find two handsome young black boys in jeans and T-shirts peering at Anna.

"Hi," she said.

The oldest boy glanced at her with eyes widened in surprise, but the younger one gave her a friendly smile. "Hi. That your baby?"

"Yes. Her name's Anna. I'm Meredith."

"I'm Lamond and I'm four." He held up the appropriate number of fingers. "This is my big brother, Jonah." He's seven.

"Nice to meet you both."

"Can your baby swim?"

With a smile, Meredith shook her head. "Not yet."

"I saw babies on TV what could swim," Lamond said matter-of-factly. "The moms and dads just put 'em in. They had a camera underneath the water so you could see 'em with their little faces all scrunched up." He demonstrated and giggled. "It was cool."

"It sounds cool," she replied. "I've heard of teaching infants to swim."

Taking a step back, he pointed toward the ocean.

"Maybe you could put her in the water and see if she can do it," he suggested.

"I'm pretty sure you'd have to teach a baby in a heated pool," she replied with a grin. "The ocean's too cold."

"It's too cold for me," Jonah said with a shudder.

"Not for me," Lamond said, puffing his chest out. "I'm tough. My dad says so."

"I'll bet you are."

"Your baby's real pretty," he said. "Can I look at her up close?"

"Sure." Meredith got out of her chair and knelt beside the baby, peeling back the blanket that protected her cheek from the elements.

Anna's rosy lips puckered and she made an instinctive little sucking motion.

"Aw." Lamond chuckled. "That's so cute."

Meredith smiled at the child who had captured her heart in record time. She thought everything Anna did was darling, too.

"D'you live around here?" Jonah asked.

"No, we're vacationing."

"Us, too," he replied. "We're staying at the Lighthouse Inn, but the only lighthouse is on the sign."

"There's a painting in the foyer," she told him. "We're staying there, too."

"We're going to see a real lighthouse," Lamond added.

"That sounds like fun."

"Are you boys bothering the lady?" The rich timbre of a male voice interrupted their discussion.

Both boys turned toward the tall man who had approached and bent to peer under the umbrella.

"We're not bothering her, Dad," Lamond said. "This is Meredith. We was just lookin' at her baby, Anna. Isn't she cute?"

Khaki trousers and a pale yellow shirt contrasted with the man's dark skin. The hands he placed on his knees as he bent forward were large, his nails blunt and pink. "She's a beauty all right," he replied with a grin. He had an energy and masculine presence that Meredith could almost feel. When he directed his attention to her, his gaze was like a physical touch.

She waited for censure in his expression...a question....

"Are these guys driving you crazy?" It wasn't the question she'd been anticipating.

His voice melted her senses like hot fudge on ice cream. "Not at all. I was glad for someone to talk to. Anna is a joy, but she doesn't have much to say."

He grinned. "Give her a couple of years and you won't be able to get a thought in edgewise."

"The voice of experience, I take it?"

He nodded good-naturedly.

"They're staying at the Lighthouse Inn, too, Dad," Lamond said.

"I guess we're neighbors, then. Temporarily anyway. Justin Weber," he introduced himself politely, "father to these two rascals."

She raised a hand and he shook it, his fingers warm, his grip firm, but gentle. The simple handshake shouldn't have given her butterflies in the pit of her stomach, but it did. "Nice to meet you."

He released her hand. Immediately, she wondered if there was a Mrs. Justin Weber, but she didn't ask because she didn't want to answer questions posed to her.

"Where's your dad?" Lamond asked.

Meredith blinked, but understood momentarily.

"Her husband you mean," Jonah corrected.

"I don't have a husband," she replied. It was a relief to be asked an easy question for a change, one she didn't mind answering. Most people asked probing questions about Anna's parentage, and Meredith found them offensive and rude.

"Did he die?" Lamond's young face took on a sad expression. "Our mom died."

The answer to her wondering was a disturbingly sad one and her heart extended even further to the motherless boys. "No, honey," she said, her voice soft with sympathy. "I never had a husband. I'm sorry about your mom."

Her gaze was drawn to the man's, but his dark one didn't reveal emotion.

"We have a nanny," Jonah said. "She's sort of like a mom."

Not knowing what to say, Meredith simply listened.

"Her name's Mauli," Lamond supplied. "It's Hawaiian. She knows how to do cartwheels."

Jonah nodded. "And she can multiply and divide in her head. Without a calculator."

"And she makes macaroni and cheese without a box." Jonah looked up at his dad. "Doesn't she, Dad?"

Justin nodded.

Meredith smiled at their exuberant praise of their nanny. "She sounds like a prize."

"Couldn't get along without her," the man said.

"Is she traveling with you?"

"Oh, yes." Justin glanced in the direction of the road that led away from the beach. "She's shopping. She gets plenty of time to herself while we're on vacation. Trips are one of her job perks."

"That's nice for her."

He nodded. "Well, boys, we'd better leave Miss…Meredith to her book and finish our walk. It was nice to meet you."

"You, too."

"We're going to see the lighthouse now," Lamond said.

"Have a good time."

"You could come with us," Lamond added, in the innocent fashion of a child. "It'll be really cool."

Again she met their father's eyes, but the man seemed a little uncomfortable this time.

She smiled. "Thank you, but I've planned to rest today. Anna and I are enjoying the beach. You have a good time."

"When we see you, we'll tell you all about it."

His innocent assumption that she would just naturally be interested in his account of their sight-seeing trip was endearing. "I'll look forward to it."

They said their goodbyes, and Justin straightened to walk away. Lamond tugged on his arm, and he swept the boy up onto his shoulders.

Meredith watched the small family as they strolled away on the tawny sand, and couldn't help noticing Justin Weber's fine form—broad shoulders, narrow hips and long legs. Sad that they'd lost their wife and mother. Nice that they were all the same color.

Whoa! Where that thought had come from, she didn't know, but she'd surprised herself with it.

Anna made tiny waking noises, and Meredith glanced at her watch. She'd planned to stay on the beach for another couple of hours, so she changed Anna and nursed her.

Occasionally someone on the beach nodded a hello, but she enjoyed the tranquility of the crashing waves and the solitude. She'd left her cell phone in her room because she didn't want Veronica to reach her and ask where she was.

Finally getting hungry, she packed up her belongings, slid Anna into the sling she wore to carry her and made her way back to the inn. As she kicked off her shoes and shook out sand at the entrance, a young male employee hurried to help her and store her beach rentals.

Meredith went to her room where she locked the door and placed Anna in the crib the inn had provided. There were four messages on her cell phone, all from Veronica, all pleading with her to call and listen to reason. Meredith deleted them, turned off her phone and took a nap.

Waking rested, she fed Anna, took a quick shower and dressed in trousers and a silky blouse. She carried Anna out to the car and glanced at the food and entertainment guide she'd discovered in a rack inside the inn. They all looked good and the addresses were meaningless, so she headed down a main street.

The first restaurant she found was a seafood place with weathered clapboard siding, a wooden walkway with posts and rope strung between them to mimic a wharf, and a shark's jawbone over the door. Meredith liked the authentic look and it had a good rating in the guidebook, so she parked and entered.

A hostess asked her seating preferences just as a young voice called, "Miss Meredith! Miss Meredith!"

She turned to discover Lamond Weber racing

across the foyer toward her. She shifted Anna's seat to her other hand. "Well, hello."

Dressed in a fresh white sport shirt, Justin walked forward and greeted her with a warm smile. "We were just being shown to a table. Will you join us?"

Meredith glanced from Justin to Lamond to the hostess and couldn't think of a single reason not to accept his offer. "Thank you. I'd love to."

"Great. We'll need another chair, miss," he said. "And one of those bases to put the car seat on."

"What's that?" Meredith asked.

He stepped beside her and touched his hand to the small of her back to guide her through the tables. She was keenly aware of his warm touch through her clothing.

"They have high chairs that flip over so you can fasten your infant seat on top," Justin explained. "Some places have an aluminum or wooden frame for the same purpose. Gets the baby up on your level, and you don't have to leave her in her seat on the floor or try to hold her while you eat."

The hostess appeared then with just such an invention and showed Meredith how to safely place Anna's carrier into the base.

"Isn't that ingenious?" Feeling like the novice she was, Meredith smiled and thanked the young woman.

In a gentlemanly gesture, Justin held Meredith's chair, then helped Lamond get settled on a booster seat.

"I take it you haven't been out to eat much since Anna's arrival," he said with a good-natured smile.

"If you don't count carryout or drive through, this is my first dinner out." She picked up a menu and glanced at the selections. The list of grilled salmon, albacore tuna and fresh salads made her mouth water.

"What's Anna going to eat?" Lamond asked.

"She won't be hungry for a while," Meredith replied. "I fed her right before we came here."

"Oh. Read me the kids' food, Dad. Please?"

Justin opened his menu and read the selection of children's dinners.

"I want the tuna melt. Can I have two?"

Justin raised an ebony brow at his son. "You're going to be growing out of all your clothes again, you keep eating so much."

Lamond giggled.

Jonah opened a backpack he'd carried in and took out two coloring books and a box of crayons. The boys settled down to color brightly hued racing cars.

Meredith thanked the waitress who set glasses of water before them. She took a sip. "What a good idea to bring along something to entertain them."

Justin had a nice smile that revealed even white teeth and disturbed her comfort level. He had a manner of looking at her that made her feel he was thinking more than he was saying. "It's either that or constantly be nagging them not to play with the silverware and the condiments. Mauli's great about picking up things to amuse them. She seems to know just what they like."

"Where is Mauli tonight?"

"Taking in a movie with a girlfriend she met yesterday."

Studying the menu, Meredith intuitively sensed stares from a nearby table and glanced in that direction. A couple with three children were seated at a round table. The youngest of the children played with an action figure on the tabletop, but the other two, a boy and girl of about seven and nine, stared at Jonah and Lamond, then at Anna in her seat and gave Meredith and Justin inquiring looks.

Their mother caught their attention and whispered something Meredith could only partially hear, but they reluctantly turned away. Meredith locked gazes with the woman momentarily, and seeming embarrassed, the young mother looked away quickly.

It was all those two children could do not to turn their heads and stare again. The woman had taken hold of the younger boy's wrist on the tabletop as though warning him.

Discomfort at being the center of attention flooded Meredith, and warmth rose in her cheeks. Her stomach dipped nervously. She glanced around to see how many other people were looking at them, but didn't notice anything unusual.

Returning her gaze to the menu but not able to

concentrate, she glanced up and found Justin studying her solemnly.

Justin had seen the children's curious gazes and
hadn't thought much of it. People probably saw them
and assumed they were a family. His boys were quite
dark-skinned, but if an onlooker thought Meredith
was his wife, then they would just quite naturally
think Anna was their child together.

He didn't really care much what people thought,
but it was apparent that Meredith did. The expression
on her face and the tilt of her chin clearly showed a
defensiveness that surprised him.

She was obviously uncomfortable with the attention
that her child—and probably Justin's company—drew.
He didn't need any complications in his life, in fact had
vowed not to take on any, but for some reason he had
the feeling that this young woman could use a friend.

Hell, everyone could use a friend. Even him—especially one this lovely. Though he surprised himself
with the thought, he admitted he wouldn't mind getting to know her better.

A whole lot better.

Three

The boys were happily coloring and hadn't noticed the curious looks they'd received. Obviously embarrassed, Meredith took a calming breath.

Justin gauged her reactions.

Meredith seemed at a loss for words, her cheeks pink, her eyes overly shiny.

"What are you feeling?" he asked softly.

"Embarrassed." She glanced to the side. "Defensive."

"Deep down?" he asked. "What are you feeling underneath all that?"

Tears welled in her eyes and she blinked, holding

her lips in a stiff line. "Disappointed. And hurt," she said softly.

They'd only just met, but he knew it had been difficult to reveal those very private feelings.

Justin nodded and studied Meredith's delicate features, her trembling lips. "Children are just naturally curious."

It was difficult enough adjusting to a new baby and the changes that a child brought to one's life, but she was apparently doing it on her own. As the mother of a half-black child, she'd no doubt already experienced her share of prejudice. She was feeling defensive with good reason. But that baby had been conceived by a black man. Hadn't she ever gone out to dinner with the baby's father, hadn't she seen people's reactions before?

She was struggling, hurting, and he didn't know whether it had been a good idea to subject her to his company and the stares that accompanied it. She hadn't seemed to mind their company on the beach, but being with other people was a different matter.

Meredith seemed tenderhearted and vulnerable, and that combination of innocence intrigued him. "I think you're extraordinarily sensitive right now," he said. "Possibly reading things into what's merely simple curiosity."

"You're probably right. Thanks."

He liked the way her smile lit up her hazel eyes.

Today they'd seemed lit by the sun, but now they were dark and almost green. "Shall we enjoy ourselves?"

She nodded, grateful for his sensible and reassuring words. When the waitress returned, Meredith ordered and Justine ordered for himself and the boys. "Would you care for wine?" he inquired.

"Thank you, but I can't," she replied. "You go ahead."

"Just a glass for me," he said to the waitress. "You're nursing," he said after she'd gone.

She nodded, a little surprised at his frankness, but not embarrassed.

"Wise choice. How do you manage when you go to work?"

"I've taken a leave of absence from my job."

"That's great. What do you do?"

"I'm a pediatric physical therapist."

One side of his lips quirked in a half smile. "No wonder you're so good with kids."

Her fair skin blushed prettily. "I love kids."

"They like you, too."

The waitress brought his wine and refilled Meredith's water glass.

"What about you?" she asked. "What do you do?"

"I'm an attorney." He raised a palm as though to ward off her reaction. "No lawyer jokes, now."

"I don't think I know any."

"That's refreshing."

"You hear a lot of lawyer jokes?"

"Uh-huh."

"Like what? Tell me one."

She was serious. He chuckled. "No."

"Not dignified enough for you, I suppose? I'm trying to picture you in your three-piece suit."

"I look pretty good."

She laughed. "You're one of those *GQ* guys, aren't you? You have a dozen suits and a hundred color-coordinated ties and matching socks."

He shrugged.

"You do. And you buy Italian shoes."

"What do you know about men's shoes?"

"I had a— Well…" She looked away. "I knew someone who liked to dress well."

The baby's father? Where was he now? What kind of man left a woman pregnant and alone or with a baby to raise by herself? Maybe he hadn't known about the baby. Maybe he'd died. Justin was certainly curious about this woman's private life, and he had no right to be. She was just an acquaintance he'd met on the beach. "Do you think my taste in shoes says something about my character?"

"Probably. But I wouldn't know what it would be. I'm not a very good judge of people."

Justin absorbed that remark silently.

Meredith glanced away, suddenly self-conscious about saying something a little too revealing.

Jonah showed his dad the picture he'd colored, and the conversation turned to sports cars, of which Meredith knew nothing, so she listened to father and sons.

Their salmon arrived with spicy slaw and mango-papaya salsa on the side, and they ate leisurely. The boys finished, pulled a miniature magnetic checker-board from Jonah's backpack and played the game.

Anna squirmed in her seat and a telltale odor rose.

Lamond wrinkled his nose. "Is *that* your baby?"

"Uh-oh," Meredith said. "Excuse us for a moment. We'll be right back."

She unbuckled Anna and carried her to the women's rest room. As she was finishing the change, the door opened and a matronly woman entered.

She glanced at Anna and her eyebrows rose indignantly. "*Where* did you *get* that baby?"

Meredith thought her lips moved a minute before she could find a response. "She's mine."

"But you're not her *mother?* Where did she come from?"

"She came from my uterus and I most definitely *am* her mother." Indignantly, Meredith stuffed the baby-wipe container in her bag, picked up Anna and closed the changing station. Those were the kind of remarks that made her suspicious of every glance she received. The kind that angered her and dented her faith in mankind.

Outside the rest room, she paused and collected herself before making her way back to the table where she placed Anna back into her seat.

The boys had packed their belongings and sat on the edges of their chairs.

Justin stood, but looked at her curiously. "I guess we're ready to go. Everything okay?"

Meredith reached into the bag to dig for her wallet. "Fine."

Justin touched his long fingers to her wrist. "I got dinner."

"You shouldn't have done that."

"It was a pleasure to have your company," he replied, then picked up the infant carrier. "I'll help you to your car."

Accepting his aid, she walked ahead of him out into the cool evening air. He seemed to be a nice guy and she wanted to believe he was as kind and sincere as he seemed. The boys jumped from the boardwalk onto the stones below and knelt to look more closely at the rocks.

Meredith's car was parked right in front, and she used her remote key ring to unlock the doors.

Justin glanced at the license plate. "You're from Oregon."

She nodded. "Portland."

That half smile inched up and creased one cheek.

"You, too?" she asked.

He nodded. "Small world, eh?"

Her mind whirled with the possibility of developing a friendship with this man, a friendship that would last once they'd both gone home.

Justin looked over the seat and the base, and efficiently buckled Anna into the car in no time.

"You're good at this," she commented.

"I've had a little practice."

"That's nice to see." She closed the back door and opened the front. "I feel like I owe you."

He glanced toward the sun setting over the ocean in the distance. "You can buy me dinner next time."

Meredith's heart felt as though it dipped in her chest. Was he suggesting a *date?*

He looked directly at her. "Do you have a problem being with me and the boys in public?"

Heat flashed through her chest and up to her cheeks. "Did you— You didn't think that I was embarrassed to be sitting with you in there." She pointed over her shoulder. "Did you?"

He raised his eyebrows and set his lips thoughtfully before speaking. "I wasn't sure. You said you were embarrassed."

Meredith glanced at the boys still selecting rocks. "Like you said, I'm extra sensitive right now." She wanted to mention the woman in the rest room, but didn't know how to put it that wouldn't sound self-pitying or be insulting to him. "I'm embarrassed to be singled out. I'm angry that Anna's skin color has to be an issue at all."

She looked up at him, silently pleading for understanding. "I wasn't embarrassed to be with you or your sons, Justin. Please don't think that."

He nodded. "Okay."

His simple word hung between them, amiable closure to a touchy subject. Its very simplicity and his acceptance of her feelings lightened her spirits and made her smile.

A breeze caught her hair and his attention focused on it for a moment, then found her eyes.

"We'll see each other again," she said, finding the words bold, but not wanting to miss the chance.

"Actually," he said, "I'd like for you to meet Mauli."

She thought about it and didn't see any reason to say no. She gave a little shrug. "All right."

"Do you have plans for tomorrow?"

"Yes, I have an important meeting with the beach. Is there rain in the forecast?"

"This is February on the coast. There's always rain in the forecast."

"I was afraid of that."

"If it's warm and clear, we'll meet on the beach. Say around one?"

She nodded. "One it is."

He turned and called to his boys. "Come on, fellas, let's go. Tell Miss Meredith good-night."

Jonah waved, but Lamond ran over to where she stood at the open car door and looked up at her. He was as endearingly straightforward and open as his father. "I think you and Anna are real nice. And pretty, too. Bye, Miss Meredith."

"Bye, sweetie." She instinctively reached out to touch his face and found his cheek as smooth and warm as Anna's.

"Step back from the car," Justin called and Lamond obeyed.

Meredith got in.

"See ya later, alligator!" Lamond called with an energetic wave.

She returned the wave and called, "After a while, crocodile!"

He broke into giggles and ran to join his father and older brother.

Meredith closed the door and started her car, a good, warm feeling replacing her earlier chagrin. She would see the Webers again tomorrow…if it didn't rain. Glancing at the sky, she turned on the radio to find a weather report.

At 6:00 a.m. when Anna woke to nurse, it was raining. Meredith settled in the comfortable chair near the bay window that overlooked a portion of the beach and watched the gray drizzle coming down. She wasn't here to socialize, anyway, she told herself with glum resign. She'd accepted the Children's Connection's offer in order to escape her mother's constant harassment and have some time alone with Anna to think.

Adoption, as her mother had insisted from day one, had never been an option. She'd wanted this baby. She'd gone to extreme measures to have her, and Anna was the fulfillment of her dreams. Just because she wasn't the particular baby Meredith had imagined didn't mean she didn't love her and want her.

Her fears were about her own inadequacies. She hadn't been prepared to raise a child of mixed race. Right now Anna's needs were simple and Meredith had the capabilities to meet them: breast milk, clean clothing, hundreds of diapers and a lot of love. But later—maybe only three or four years from now—her daughter would begin to recognize the differences in their appearance. She would notice the stares and hear the comments and need skills to cope. And how would Meredith know how to instill those tools, give her child the confidence and sense of identity she would need?

Whenever Meredith gave in to those thoughts, she sank into a pit of self-doubt and insecurity.

During Anna's wakeful time, she bathed her, sang her nursery songs and admired her toothless new smile.

Her main dilemma was the question of responsibility. No, she did not want to sue the clinic. But neither did she want a terrible mistake to be made again—perhaps to someone who couldn't accept their unexpected child.

She could probably discover who the sperm donor was, but in her heart she didn't want to know. It couldn't possibly matter. The one thing she knew with confidence was that she had to be certain her own eggs were used in the in vitro process. In her heart Anna was her own child and always would be. She'd carried her inside her body, underneath her heart, and had gone through the birth process. Anna was her baby. But was she truly her *biological* child? If one mistake was made, why not another?

Time and again she stared at her child, trying to find similarities in appearance, wanting more than anything to see physical traits. But Anna was a baby. A dark-skinned baby. And it was difficult to tell.

While Anna slept, Meredith checked her voice mail and deleted all the messages from Veronica without listening to them. Then she called her counselor at Children's Connection.

"I need assurance that my own eggs were fertilized and implanted. I don't care about the donor. I don't want to know and I don't want anyone else to ever be able to find out."

"I understand perfectly," the woman said. "I'll check all the paper trails and I'll call you when I have an answer."

Already feeling less burdened, Meredith hung up and gave herself a manicure and pedicure, using a bright shade of red nail polish she'd received in a basket of personal items as a gift from her friend Chaney.

Thinking of the bubbly redhead, Meredith glanced at the clock and called her friend's cell phone, hoping Chaney had it turned on where she worked at a medical billing company in Portland.

Chaney answered the phone. "Hey, it's about time you called."

"I've been settling in."

"How's the Lighthouse Inn?"

"It's marvelous. I have a huge suite with a bay window and a balcony that's only a few hundred feet from the beach. There's a whirlpool tub and a little kitchen."

"Been in the whirlpool yet?"

"Not yet. It's an executive suite decked out so well that a person could live here."

"I figured it would be pretty classy. They're trying to buy you off."

"You're probably right. But I couldn't pass up the chance to escape for a while."

"She's called me twice a day demanding I tell her where you are."

Meredith knew Chaney referred to her mother. "Don't cave, Chaney."

"Never. She needs to give you some breathing room. How's my favorite girl?"

"Anna's perfectly content. She doesn't care where we are. She eats and sleeps oblivious to anything but her tummy and her bottom. I think she's becoming partial to my singing, however."

"Nah, she still likes my rendition of 'Lonely Days, Lonely Nights' the best. I got her first smile with that one."

"You did not."

"Did so. You'll have to stay up nights practicing to outdo my performances."

Meredith laughed. "Okay, okay, you're probably a micrometer better at entertaining in that department. But I can feed her. Thank God."

"Low blow, girlfriend."

They laughed, and Meredith said, "I needed this. You keep me centered and laughing at myself."

"Yeah, well, sometimes you have to laugh."

Meredith glanced at the windows, then at the clock. It was nearly one. "The sun is shining! I'd better let you go back to work."

"Call me tomorrow."

"I will. Bye."

Four

Justin and his boys were waiting on the beach, the sand darkened from the morning's rain. With them was a young woman in her early twenties, with dark hair and tanned-looking skin. The closer Meredith got, the more she noticed about the girl. She doubted that was a tan; her skin was a little darker than Anna's, but her hair was straight and her eyes blue. She was quite obviously of mixed race.

She smiled and peered into the sling to see the napping baby.

"Meredith, this is Mauli," Justin said. "Mauli, this is the lady and the baby we told you about."

"The boys couldn't stop talking about your Anna,"

Mauli said. "They said she was the cutest thing ever, and I have to agree."

"Thanks. I'm partial, but I agree, too."

"It's really too wet to spend time on the beach this afternoon," Justin said, disappointing Meredith.

She nodded in agreement, however.

"I thought we'd find something else to do," he suggested. "Spend some time seeing the sights. Will you join us?"

Warm relief swept over her at his suggestion. She shouldn't be reliant on others for a good time, but she'd eagerly been looking forward to today. Justin and the kids were so accepting and friendly. They didn't know about her dilemma or have opinions about what she needed to do. She could relax and enjoy herself around them. "I'd love it."

"Great. We'll take my vehicle."

"Are we going to see the whales and dolphins, Dad?" Lamond tugged on his father's hand.

"No, that's tomorrow, remember?"

Justin led them to a Lexus SUV with a cherry sheen so deep it was almost black. "Give me your keys and I'll get Anna's car seat. Do you have a stroller in your trunk?"

Meredith dug her keys from her bag. He returned quickly and fastened Anna's carrier in the rear seat, facing backward. If this man was as efficient in court as he was with babies, he was a force to be reckoned with.

They all piled in and buckled up. Meredith chatted with Mauli while Justin drove south on the highway. Mauli had been frequenting the gift shops in the little beach town and described the delightful presents she was storing away for Christmas and birthdays.

When Justin parked, it was at a wharf area, and they got out. Their first stop was the public rest room in a charming cluster of shops built to look as though they'd been there a hundred years. While Meredith changed Anna, Justin unfolded the stroller he'd stored in the back of his vehicle. Lamond asked to push it, but Justin told him that was Meredith's job.

Funnel cakes caught Lamond's attention next, so Justin bought enough to go around.

"You're a bad influence," she said as the boys ran ahead and Mauli hurried after them. "I don't usually eat this stuff."

Justin leaned toward her and brushed powdered sugar from her chin. Her heart skittered at the touch and at his attention. Her reaction surprised her.

"Yeah, I'm bad to the bone," he replied. "Watch yourself. I might suggest ice cream later."

She laughed and felt Justin's warm gaze.

"That's a nice sound," he said.

Warmth bloomed in her cheeks and she glanced aside.

Justin shifted his attention ahead. "Turn up here, fellas."

After they'd turned right, a fantasyland of metal sculptures came into view, some intricate, some sturdier, all of them turning and spinning in the wind. Meredith's attention was riveted. "Oh, my!"

"Isn't it great? I kicked myself for not getting one of these last year. This time I'm buying something for myself and having one shipped to my mom, as well."

Jonah and Lamond wound through the display of art. "Dad, I like this one!" the younger boy called.

Justin went to study the sculptures with his sons.

"Come on," Mauli said to Meredith. "The guy who designs them works inside this building. If we're lucky, he'll be making something."

Sure enough a tall young man in a cap was seated at a bench pounding metal into hollow shapes the size of half baseballs. He looked up. "Hi, ladies."

They watched as he shaped half a dozen of the cups, all the while talking about his craft. He then fastened the cups to a frame that looked like a small windmill. It already had a dozen or more of the wind catchers attached. Finally he placed the whole piece before a huge fan. When he turned it on, the gadget came to life, smoothly rotating in the breeze.

Justin and the boys had entered the shop, and the boys made appreciative exclamations.

"I like that one, Dad!" Lamond said.

"You like all of them," Justin replied with a laugh.

"But I like that one the best."

"I do, too." He turned to the artist. "Can I pay for that one and when it's ready have it shipped to my home address?"

"No problem," the man replied. He pushed an intercom button. "My wife'll come down and take care of the details."

"Now let's find one for your grandma," he said to the boys, and they began a new search.

Meredith pushed Anna's stroller back outside and admired the metal sculptures, wondering if she'd regret not buying one today. It would be fun to have one in her yard as a remembrance of the ocean breezes.

She decided on a piece with six long, delicate, gently curving arms, the wind cups fashioned like shells and a counterweight on the opposite side of the wheel. As the wind caught it, the arms spun the shells in a whirl of shining metal. Pleased with her choice, she went inside and paid for her purchase.

"It's only a few dollars more to ship two together," the short, friendly faced wife of the artist said. "Unless you need priority or express shipping?"

Meredith blinked, turning the words over in her mind. "I only want one, thanks."

"Your husband is having one shipped home, too, dear. Oh my, you haven't disagreed on which one to get, have you?"

The woman's assumption came clearly into focus. "I, uh, we're not—"

Justin came to her rescue. "No, we want both of ours sent to the same address. I don't need priority delivery, do you?"

She shook her head. "No."

"We'll save a few bucks on shipping this way," he said to her. "I'll bring yours over when they arrive. That okay?"

She nodded. "Sure."

Purchases and delivery confirmed, they walked outside.

Meredith didn't know what to say. The woman had assumed they were married.

"It's okay," Justin said to her. "It's perfectly natural for a casual observer to assume we're a couple, since we're shopping and sight-seeing as what must look like a family. I'm sorry if you're embarrassed."

"I'm not embarrassed," she replied, almost defensively.

"Then there's no problem."

"None whatsoever."

"Then let's continue our holiday."

He walked forward and she caught up to him.

Their next tour was of a boatyard. The owners built reproductions of rowboats and fishing boats dating back to the 1800s, and all the boats were available to rent and take out on the water.

"I'll try this one," Justin said, pointing to a particular rowboat bobbing on the calm inlet. "Who's coming with me?"

Jonah and Lamond ran forward, but Mauli hung back. She glanced at Meredith and shuddered. "I don't think I want to be on the ocean in a boat that small with those two kids jumping around. You go ahead, though. I'll stay here with Anna."

Meredith shook her head. Anna was awake and fussing. "I'll just sit here with you, thanks." She called across the distance, "We'll stay here. Have fun."

He and the boys scrambled into the boat and Justin rowed out in the water.

Meredith and Mauli bought drinks and sat at a round table with an umbrella. Gulls swooped nearby, pecked at the ground then flew off.

Meredith placed a receiving blanket over her shoulder, took Anna from her stroller and opened her nursing bra to place the baby at her breast. "So you're a student?"

Mauli nodded. "I'm in my third year."

"What's your major?"

"Ethnic studies. African-American history last year."

Meredith's interest picked up. "Do you want to teach?"

"Teach or counsel. Kids probably."

"Big surprise."

Mauli smiled. "Yeah, I like kids." She sipped her

soft drink and glanced at Meredith. "You haven't asked. My dad is black and my mother is white and Hawaiian. In Hawaiian, my name means dark-skinned."

"I wouldn't have asked."

"You've heard a lot of questions about Anna, haven't you?"

Meredith nodded.

Mauli set her paper cup on the table. "I've heard them all. And so have my parents."

"Some of them are so…hurtful."

"Yes," Mauli agreed. "But some are just thoughtlessly curious."

"I guess so."

"People get uncomfortable when they can't easily categorize you."

Meredith thought over the girl's remarks.

"There are five standard racial pigeonholes," she said, holding up one hand. "If you don't fit, you stand out. Probably the questions I heard the most while growing up were 'Is that your dad?', 'Is that your mom?' and 'Are you adopted?'"

Meredith imagined what it must feel like for a child to hear those questions. "Last night a woman asked me where this baby came from," she told Mauli, revealing something she'd never thought she would have shared. "The question makes it seem as though Anna is an alien or something."

Saying the words aloud made her head buzz for a

few seconds, but it was liberating to get the frustration off her chest.

Mauli studied the shop fronts and the few passing tourists. "Four-point-five million kids under eighteen in this country are multiracial," she said matter-of-factly, impressing Meredith with her knowledge. "In some areas one out of six babies born is of two or more racial heritages. Multiracial youth is one of the fastest growing segments of our population."

"I guess numbers don't necessarily mean acceptance, do they?" Meredith asked.

"I would love to unscrew the top of people's heads and zap racism with a magic laser. That and the obsessive need to put everyone in a category." The young woman's voice held a note of wistfulness, but not the anger with which Meredith struggled.

Meredith had never before had a straightforward conversation like this with anyone except Chaney, and Mauli's insights touched her.

"Acceptance really has to be here," Mauli said, touching her fingers to her shirt over her heart. "Acceptance of one's self first. Because fitting in is a challenge. But knowing who you are is the key."

Meredith's throat tightened with anxiety for her child. She felt so incapable of being able to teach those things to her child that it frightened her. "I'm afraid I won't know how to help Anna," she managed to say as she moved Anna to her other breast.

"There are plenty of people to help you," Mauli assured her. "I belong to a couple of college organizations now. As long as you're willing to help her explore her racial heritage, there is guidance available."

Mauli was wise beyond her years. "If I was underhanded, I'd steal you away from Justin to be Anna's nanny."

Mauli laughed. "Now that would take some doing. But we live in the same town, right? I can sure be your friend."

Emotion welled up in Meredith's chest and tears blurred her vision. "Thank you. You're the first person I've talked to who's given me hope that I can actually do this."

"Someday I hope you can meet my mom and dad," Mauli said, handing her a paper napkin.

Meredith blotted her tears. "Where are they?"

"They live in West Virginia right now. My dad's in the air force."

"Well, you've dealt with it all, military upbringing, as well. New schools and all that."

Mauli nodded. "Name a state with an air base. I've probably lived there."

Anna had finished nursing and Meredith adjusted her clothing. Mauli asked to hold the baby.

Meredith hadn't been paying much attention to the guys, but turned now to watch them returning to shore.

Justin was rowing smoothly and both boys were sitting at his feet. "He's a great dad," she said, thinking aloud.

Mauli agreed. "The best."

"Do you know how his wife died?"

"A freak thing," she replied. "A bridge collapsed and her car was on the interstate beneath it. The people in the car behind hers were killed, too. She was on her way back from shopping. Started out as a regular day, I guess."

"How awful."

"I never knew her. Justin hired me about a month later. The boys were still small and all of them were grieving."

"You must have been a big help to them."

"I hope so. Actually it's like being in a family. I have a place to live while I go to school, and I get paid to do laundry, shop and supervise the kids. It's good for all of us."

An attendant helped Justin pull the boat into its moor, and the boys scrambled out and ran toward the women. "That was cool!" Jonah cried, uncharacteristically vocal. "Did you see Lamond almost tip the boat over?"

"We must have missed that," Mauli responded. She leaned toward Meredith. "Now you know why I stayed on shore."

Justin joined them. "I worked up an appetite. Who's hungry?"

Jonah and Lamond responded noisily. With Anna on her shoulder, Mauli said, "It's early enough to beat the crowds for supper."

"Let's go." Justin herded them back to his Lexus and drove until he spotted a family restaurant.

He took charge of getting a table and ushering everyone into seats. Meredith was shamelessly enjoying being pampered.

"Dad, there's a game room," Jonah said after they'd ordered. "Can we have some quarters?"

Justin took a few one-dollar bills out of his wallet. "At the counter ask very politely for change."

"Thanks."

The boys took off and Mauli followed, leaving Meredith and Justin alone, except for the sleeping baby.

Five

"Did you enjoy the afternoon?" Justin asked.

"Very much." The waitress had brought her a club soda with a lemon slice on the rim of the glass, and she sipped the iced drink. "Thank you for introducing me to Mauli."

"I thought you'd like meeting her."

"You knew I needed encouragement."

"Everyone needs encouragement."

"You know what I mean."

He threaded his long fingers together and placed his elbows on the table, looking at her thoughtfully. "I know."

She could only imagine what he was wondering

about her single-parent status. He was so straightforward, she wished she could share more with him. It
was too much to go into so soon, and besides, she
was enjoying her anonymity. "I chose to be a single
parent."

"I see. I imagined a guy who didn't want to deal
with fatherhood and cut out."

She shook her head. "There was a guy once. But
it wasn't fatherhood he couldn't deal with. I'm better off without him."

"Probably. But you're wary."

"Yes."

"And maybe that's partly why you chose to have
a child alone. You didn't trust a man to stick
around."

Bingo. "Maybe."

"So a man would really have to earn your trust to
get anywhere with you."

She didn't have a reply, and she didn't know if he
was suggesting something or not, so she shrugged
noncommittally.

"Tell me about your life," he said. "Your family
and your job."

She waved a hand. "I don't want to talk about my
family. My job is great. As you know I work with
children recovering from accidents or surgeries who
have disabilities. I see a lot of special-needs kids. A
couple of years ago, I got this idea that I wanted to

start a camp for them, and call it Camp I Can. Some of those children want so badly to do normal things and be treated as equals."

"What type of medical problems do these kids face?"

"The whole gamut. Kidney and liver transplants, leukemia and cancer among other things."

Justin nodded thoughtfully. "We're so fortunate."

She leaned forward. "Creating something for these kids became my personal goal. I was fund-raising and doing a pretty good job of it until…well, until I had a few personal setbacks. Then the camp idea took a back seat to my pregnancy and Anna's birth. But I'm ready to get involved again."

"I'm sure you'll be able to pull it off. I can hear the passion in your voice."

"I plan to return to work and get back to this project as soon as my vacation here is over."

"How long are you here for?"

"Two weeks."

"We've come to this beach for three years now," Justin said. "When my wife was alive we used to go to Florida to see her family. Now I send the boys for a week twice a year to visit their grandparents. It's too difficult for me to go back there."

"A lot of memories?" she asked softly.

"Too many." He propped his chin on a knuckle for a moment. "I met my wife in college, and we married when I graduated. She postponed the rest of her schooling to work while I clerked for next to nothing. We lived in a tiny little place. I landed better and better jobs, but by then Jonah had come along and then Lamond.

"Kayla didn't need to work anymore, but she didn't go back to school, either. She said there was plenty of time for that." He paused and Meredith felt the bone-deep sadness in his exhalation. "But she ran out of time. One day everything changed and her life was over." He looked away for a moment, then turned back. "It was an accident."

"Mauli told me."

"Kayla wanted to be an engineer. She'd have been brilliant."

"She had what she really wanted," Meredith told him. "She chose to be a wife and a mother and to stay home with her children. Sometimes a person's ambitions change when her life takes an unexpected turn. Like meeting the right person. I doubt that she was unfulfilled."

He paused before saying, "She said she was happy. But she should have had more time."

Instinct carried Meredith's hand across the table to cover his. "Yes, she should have. And you have every right to think her death was unfair."

"I've worked really hard to keep us a family. And Mauli was a godsend." He noticed her hand then, and turned his over so that their palms touched. He glanced up into her eyes. "I've gotten morose and I apologize. I try not to do that."

"Please don't apologize. It's good to be able to talk about things. All of life isn't perfect and there's no good in pretending it is."

"Can I be honest with you?" he asked.

She nodded. "Of course."

"When we met yesterday, I sensed you needed a friend. I was hoping to be that. And I knew Mauli could be a friend, too. Instead, you're turning out to be a friend to me."

"Isn't that what friendships are? Two-sided?"

He squeezed her hand and released it. "I've been too busy to cultivate many friendships," he admitted. "So I'm not an authority."

"Well, I have one very good friend."

He raised a curious brow.

"Her name is Chaney and I've known her since college. She's daring and funny and quite nonconforming. She makes me laugh and keeps me from getting too serious about myself."

"She sounds like a great person." He fixed her with an inquisitive stare. "Now describe Meredith in a few words, just like you did Chaney."

She sat back in her chair thoughtfully. "Meredith is…cautious and prepared…and tenderhearted, but purposeful." Rather pleased with herself, she smiled. "That was interesting."

He grinned.

"What about you?"

He took a deep breath. "Justin is…well prepared, efficient and takes initiative. Charming, too. Can't forget that."

"Goes without saying."

"I said it."

"You're thorough, as well."

They laughed. Then sobered and glanced at each other a little awkwardly, their awareness of each other needing more time and discovery. The discomfort passed as soon as Justin's half smile inched up.

"Where are *your* folks?" she asked. "You haven't mentioned them."

"They live in Dallas. We visit them a couple of times a year."

A few minutes later the boys and Mauli returned and their meals were served. Anna uncannily chose that moment to wake and squirm in her seat.

When Meredith moved toward her, Justin stopped her. "You eat, and I'll hold her. When you're finished, I'll eat."

"But your food will get cold."

"Won't be the first time. I'll ask the waitress to reheat it. No argument. Eat."

Anna always got fussy at dinnertime, but at home, Meredith simply worked around it. But now it was nice to have Justin's help. She'd have to add *consid-*

erate and *intuitive* to his list of good qualities, she thought, and smiled to herself.

"Private joke?" he asked.

She nodded.

Much later, after Justin had eaten, they left the restaurant. It was still early, and he drove along the highway, stopping once at an exit with an observation tower. They climbed the wooden stairs and breathlessly enjoyed a panoramic view of the coast, a craggy shoreline and a lighthouse in the foggy distance.

"I'd never have done all this by myself," Meredith said as they reached Cannon Beach. She was sitting in the back seat with Mauli, Anna's seat between them. "Thank you for inviting me."

Justin caught her gaze in the rearview mirror. "Thanks for going."

She noticed Mauli glance at her and Justin, then discreetly look out her side window.

Justin grinned, and in the mirror, Meredith saw his eyes crinkle.

Sometimes, like during their earlier conversation, she thought they were developing a friendship— and they were. But other times—like just now—she detected flirting and her silly heart responded spontaneously.

She didn't have room in her life for anything serious. But flirting? Well, flirting she could probably handle—and definitely enjoy.

The sun had set by the time they reached the Lighthouse Inn. Justin parked the Lexus and the doors were thrust open.

Meredith carried Anna around to the rear, waiting for him to open the back and unload her stroller. Mauli and the boys called goodbyes and headed for the front doors.

Justin surprised her by leaning against the bumper.

She looked at him.

"Be foolish to move everything if we're going to need it again tomorrow," he said.

Still she studied him.

"Will you join us on our excursion to see the whales?"

Meredith's heart fluttered nervously.

"Do you need more time alone?" he asked. "Or can we enjoy our vacations together? It's more fun this way—for me, anyway."

"You're not just taking pity on me?" She was being serious. She didn't need anyone feeling sorry for her. She did just fine on her own.

"Don't know what there is to pity," he replied.

"Right." She hadn't told him much, had she? She was enjoying living in the here and now. "Okay. Tomorrow. What time?"

"We're leaving at nine."

"I'll be ready."

"Be sure to dress warm and bundle up Anna." He

walked her up the path and through the entrance into the lobby. "Where's your room?"

She nodded toward one of the wings. "That way."

"We're upstairs."

Turning to walk down the hall, she smiled and waved. "See you tomorrow."

With the door locked and Anna tucked safely into the crib, Meredith undressed and showered, letting the soothing hot water sluice over her to relax her tired muscles and clear her mind. Setting her towel aside, she opened the basket of goodies from Chaney and un-screwed the lid from a bottle of emollient body lotion.

The delicious scent drifted upward as she rubbed it into her skin. Coffee? Meredith glanced at the bot-tle. Cappuccino, no less. Leave it to Chaney. Steam evaporated from the mirror in uneven patches, reveal-ing parts of her body. Her waist wasn't bad; she'd done hours of Pilates getting her shape back after An-na's birth. Her left breast came into view, fuller than her pre-baby form and swollen.

The mirror cleared and her right breast appeared, smaller than the other because it produced less milk. Two pink scars, both about three inches long, and the slight disfiguration were physical reminders that she was a survivor. Reminders she didn't need. Not a day went by that Meredith didn't think of herself as a sur-vivor, and thanked God and technology and made a mental note to enjoy life to the fullest.

She'd been engaged once. The thought still brought an ache to her chest when she remembered how Sean had deserted her after he'd learned that she had cancer. So much for true love, for the whole in-sickness-and-in-health bit. She'd told herself a million times it was better she'd learned Sean's true nature before she'd married him.

She wasn't ashamed of the scars. She was proud of her victory. But she was afraid.

Afraid that a man would never look at her without pity or revulsion. Afraid that she'd never again have an intimate relationship.

Afraid that life would never be as full as she'd hoped.

Six

"*Cappuccino* body lotion, Chaney?"

"Isn't it yummy?"

"Definitely, but I've been craving a latte since last night."

"Order up a decaf."

"You know it still has a jillion calories."

"Kiddo, you came through breast cancer with flying colors, I don't think a few calories are going to kill you."

"I'll stick with my juice and milk and an occasional black decaf, thank you."

"You party animal."

She sank onto the bed and traced the sailboat pattern on the coverlet with her index finger. "Hey, I'm eating for two."

"So am I. Drinking for two, as well, and I've never even been pregnant."

Meredith laughed at her friend's quirky humor.

"So what are you doing there by yourself all day? Isn't the beach cold this time of year?"

"It's not bad. Anna and I have our fleece jackets."

"Oh, yeah, that pink-and-white number that makes her look like Neapolitan ice cream."

"Food again," Meredith complained with a chuckle. "You're comparing my child to food."

"So you wear your jackets and what, watch seagulls?"

"Are you kidding? This place is a hopping tourist town. Yesterday we went for a ride up the coast and browsed through some wonderful shops. I bought a wind gizmo—you'll love it. Then for dinner ate at a terrific restaurant. The salmon here is out of this world."

"And you don't mind touristing and eating by yourself?"

"Well…I wasn't alone for dinner, actually."

"Really."

"Or for the road trip, either," she confessed. "I met a family vacationing at the same inn."

"Oh?"

"Yes, they're from Portland, too."

"Middle-aged couple with kids or something?"

Meredith got up and walked to the window, where she looked past the parking area and down a ways to the beach. The morning sun glistened on the sand. "No. Justin is a widower. He has two small boys, and their nanny is with them. Her name's Mauli, and she's a college student. She's a gem."

"Meredith Malone. You were holding out on me!"

"I didn't want you to get the wrong idea."

"What, that you're spending time with a single guy? How old is he? Is he hot? On a scale of one to ten."

"It's strictly a family thing. We're combining our little families to see the sights." She paused. "He's in his thirties, and he's…well, he's a nine-and-a-half."

"You wouldn't have given him a nine-and-a-half if you weren't interested," Chaney argued. "Sean was only an eight and you were engaged to him."

"He was an eight because he had those funny little ears."

"Justin, huh? How tall is he?"

"Six foot or better."

"Eyes?"

"Brown."

"Good smile?"

Meredith turned back into the room and sank onto the bed again. "*Great* smile. He does this half-smile thing, where just one side of his mouth turns up and it creases his cheek." She flopped backward. "God, it's sexy."

"Uh-huh. Just a family thing, my chubby booty. Is he interested?"

"I don't know. Sometimes I think so and other times I think I'm just imagining things."

"What kind of things?"

"A little flirting maybe. That smile."

"What are you doing today?"

"Whale watching."

"Cool. Call me with the details tonight. And, Mer?"

"Yeah?"

"Have fun."

"I will." She turned off the phone, noting the time and left it on the desk as she had the day before. She finished dressing, pulled her hair into a ponytail and packed Anna's diaper bag.

By the time she was ready and had toted Anna and her paraphernalia to the foyer, the Webers were waiting for her, dressed in their warm jackets. Mauli reached for Anna and Justin took the other things, so Meredith followed behind with the boys. It was becoming second nature to accompany them, and the luxury of having help was pure bliss.

This time the boys took the far rear area where they played with toy cars, and Mauli sat beside the baby in the middle, so Meredith sat up front with Justin.

"Did you have a good night?" he asked.

She nodded. "Anna's getting so she only wakes once during the night, and after she's fed she goes right back to sleep."

"And she's only three months? That's great."

"I'm really fortunate," she replied. "In so many ways."

Justin put a CD in the player and music filtered through the interior of the vehicle. "Our charter leaves at ten," he said. "I made the reservations ahead, just in case it was a busy day. We'll get there a little early and stake out our positions."

"Have you done this before?" she asked.

"Once during the migrating season in March. It was phenomenal."

"Now isn't a good time?"

"It's a good time. March is best, but some pods of whales are residents and stay near the coast all year, so you see them anytime. And this is a much better season for the boat trip, because the water is so choppy earlier in winter."

She grimaced. "I'd pass, then."

Justin found the harbor where the charter service was located and parked in the lot. Mauli unbuckled Anna and handed her to Meredith, while Justin got the boys from the back.

He indicated a small shingled building. "I'll be right back."

"Justin," she said, "I need to pay for my trip."

"It's a group fare," he said, walking away. "My treat."

She turned around and glanced at Mauli who just shrugged.

Within a few minutes, Justin returned with their tickets. As he was explaining the boarding procedure, the boat's horn blew, sending a ripple of anticipation up Meredith's spine. Jonah and Lamond, obviously equally excited, took off at a run, and Justin called for them to wait.

The Sandpiper was a deluxe sixty-five-foot excursion boat with two viewing decks and inside seating for nearly fifty people. There were only about half that many on today's cruise, leaving plenty of room to roam about and select choice seating.

They stood on deck in the warm sun as the boat pulled out into the harbor. Guides in bright orange jackets gave talks on the sea life and answered questions.

About forty-five minutes into their trip, Anna grew hungry and chewed on her fist.

"I'm going to sit inside for a while and feed her," Meredith said.

"Want some company?" Justin asked.

"Well, sure."

He guided her up a short set of stairs and they found seating near the front window. Justin observed the ocean while Meredith got Anna settled and herself modestly draped.

"I thought it would be a lot colder," she said, letting him know it was safe to turn and join her.

"We managed to plan our vacations during a good stretch of weather," he replied. "Well, mine had been postponed by a couple of weeks, so I guess it turned out for the best."

"What was the delay?"

"Things kept coming up at work. I had a fire settlement to handle, and finally got that sewn up."

"Arson?"

"No, insurance."

"So you're not a criminal or divorce lawyer."

He shook his head. "Corporate law."

"Like *The Practice*?"

"I know that's a television show, but when I have time, I'm more of a *CSI* fan."

She turned her attention toward the expanse of water.

From somewhere behind them, a female guide pointed out a few harbor seals. Then the boat slowed and came to a stop.

"Captain must've spotted a whale." Justin stood and stepped close to the window ledge and peered out at the ocean.

The tourists aboard the boat murmured their excitement and Meredith looked out at the expanse of water in time to see a gray whale breaching. The sight was amazing, but it was Justin as he sat down beside her who set her heart beating faster.

She glanced down at the deck, where the boys were jumping excitedly, Mauli standing devotedly beside them. "You're fortunate to have Mauli."

"Yes. I am. You might want to give a thought to finding a nanny for Anna."

"I've already taken a few months leave from my job," she told him. "I'd love to have a live-in, but my budget won't allow for it."

"What will you do when you go back to work?"

"Take her to the day care at the hospital where I work. That way I'll be close by and can feed her on my lunch breaks. My dad offered to help out other times."

"Is your dad a widower?"

Warmth crept into Meredith's cheeks, and she didn't want to admit or discuss Veronica. "No. My mother's very much alive. She's just not the nurturing type."

If he suspected there was more that she wasn't saying, he didn't let on.

Anna had finished nursing, and Meredith adjusted her clothing and held her to her shoulder. Justin extended both hands. "May I?"

Meredith handed Anna over.

He seemed quite at ease with the infant, cradling her in one arm and gazing down at her. She studied him back, intently, her brows drawn into a frown of concentration, her dewy lips forming an O.

"You sure are a pretty little thing, Anna," he told her, touching a long finger to her chin. "Your mama will have to chase the boys off with a stick."

Anna's expression crinkled into a beaming, toothless smile, and Justin chuckled.

An ache yawned in Meredith's chest, a sad yearning for the father she hadn't thought important only a year ago. She'd planned this baby, known she was going to raise her alone and had been prepared to be the only parent her child needed.

But that had been before. Before Anna had been born and Meredith had been faced with raising a child of mixed race. Before Veronica had rejected this precious baby. Before she'd seen Justin Weber with his children—and with Anna in his arms.

It wasn't as though there would never be a man in Anna's life, she chided herself. There would be friends and Anna's grandfather. But what about a father figure? her mind nagged her belatedly. That hadn't been an issue for Meredith in the planning stages. She'd wanted a baby so badly that she'd figured no father was better than a jerk.

Justin reached across the space separating them and touched a finger between her brows. "What's the frown doing on *that* pretty face?"

Her skin warmed like a schoolgirl's.

He chuckled. "I get a kick out of seeing you turn pink like that."

Meredith looked into his face, so different from hers, so darkly handsome and intriguingly expressive, and admitted a monumental truth to herself: she felt an attraction to this man. A fascination. Something strong and exhilarating. And physical.

A sexual awareness she hadn't anticipated.

She was completely out of her comfort zone.

It felt…incredible.

Seven

Terrence Logan faced the Children's Connection's board of directors with dread. It was no ordinary appointment, what with his wife, Leslie, sitting in on the meeting, as well as the other guest in their midst.

Leslie gave her husband a supportive nod, her eyes infinitely sad with the knowledge of this problem that touched her at the core of her being.

"You're all wondering why I've called this special meeting," he said once cups were filled with coffee and the members were seated expectantly.

"I hope it's good news regarding Mr. Weber's progress with the Malone woman," Albert Squires said, fingering a cigar he had taken from the breast pocket of his burgundy suit, but wouldn't light until he'd exited the office building.

Terrence didn't want to tell them he hadn't even raised the subject of Meredith Malone with Justin yet, so he took the conversation in another direction. "I'm afraid the Malone situation is going to look like small potatoes compared to what we have to tell you today," he said on a tired exhalation.

He turned to the tall, black-haired, blue-eyed director of the Children's Connection who sat beside him. "You all know Morgan Davis."

"Out with it already," John Reynolds said.

Morgan looked from one face to the next, then gave the board the details. "One of the hospital's nurses, a woman by the name of Nancy Allen, has gone to the police with her suspicions about a black-market baby ring operating out of Children's Connection and Portland General."

The reaction was a collective inhalation followed by stunned silence.

"Miss Allen came to me last month, and I found her fears and observations worth investigating," Morgan said. "After some initial checking I met with the Logans and we called the police."

"Last month! Why weren't we told about this sooner?" Dianna March demanded.

Terrence spoke up then. "We had to be certain

that an investigation was warranted," he said. "We didn't want to set out unprepared and make a mistake that could potentially harm the reputation of Children's Connection."

"The police agreed that there were grounds for an investigation," Morgan continued. "So the FBI has been called in."

Murmurs erupted around the table.

"What exactly are they looking into?" Miles Remington asked. "What prompted this Allen woman's suspicions?"

"The Sanders kidnapping last month," Garnet Kearn guessed aloud.

Terrence nodded. "The baby the Summerses were going to adopt. There is reason to believe someone inside Children's Connection or the hospital is behind the child's disappearance."

"Is this Allen woman credible?" Wayne Thorpe asked.

Morgan ran a hand through his hair and fielded the question. "Miss Allen hesitated to do anything to damage the reputation of Children's Connection, but she's convinced that to protect any more children from the same fate, the truth must be found. Her motivation is the safety of the children. And I'm sure we all agree."

"That's not all, however." Terrence glanced from person to person. "The FBI knows for certain that the black market is working in Russia and the U.S., and now they're considering the possibility that the incidents with Elizabeth Duncan were somehow connected."

He referred to one of their adoptive parents who had traveled with an agency representative to Russia to adopt a baby in June and while there met with several disturbing attempts to kidnap her new daughter.

Oliver Pearson cleared his throat. "Of course we hold the children's safety of utmost importance," he said. "But we also have to consider the threat to Children's Connection and the hospital if these suspicions are founded."

"The most important thing is that we cooperate with the FBI investigation," Terrence said. "We all want the Sanders baby returned and the criminal apprehended."

He slanted a glance at his wife, and their eyes met in an exchange of grief and resolve. Not a person around the table was unaware of how close this situation was to the Logans' hearts. Over twenty-five years ago their child, Robbie, had been kidnapped and later found dead.

"Even if the investigation goes public," Leslie Logan said, "we will have done our part in catching the criminals. Not a one of you could justify a secret that would only aid these kidnappings."

"All the more reason that we have to put this Malone thing to rest," John Reynolds said. "We can't have that lawsuit hanging over our heads at the same time this nightmare is unfolding. It will be our un-doing if both hit the media. Our benefactors would leave us high and dry."

"How is Weber doing with Meredith Malone?" Dianna March asked. "She was pleased to accept our offer of the suite and expenses."

Terrence turned a gold fountain pen in his fingers. "We've let things develop on their own until now," he said. "Perhaps it's time someone spoke with Justin."

"Damn right it's time," Oliver said. "We need to know where she stands and we need to know soon. Things are in such a sorry state around here that we're going to have to do some fast talking to keep our butts from being raked over the coals."

Every eye in the room turned to Terrence.

He nodded his assent. "I'll call him tonight."

"Watch Anna's eyes," Lamond said, giggling. He dangled the stuffed blue dolphin above Anna's head, and her eyes widened as she followed its movements.

They had stopped for hot chocolate and souvenirs, and were seated on white painted benches in a down-town courtyard.

"There's a kite shop across the street," Justin said. "Shall we fly kites on the beach this afternoon?"

A duet of cheers went up from the boys. Mauli and Meredith simply nodded in a less exuberant show of agreement.

A few hours later, Justin and Meredith put the finishing touches to the third kite—three because the boys insisted Anna have one. Mauli sat beneath the umbrella with Anna, reading. "Do you want to fly Anna's kite?" Meredith called to her.

She shook her head. "You go ahead. I'm at a good part."

Jonah's whale kite was the first in the air. He had selected the kite after *The Sandpiper*'s captain had let him steer the boat that morning and teasingly commented that they had to keep a careful eye out for anyone named Jonah on a whale watch.

Justin helped Lamond with his dinosaur kite while Meredith ran along the beach with Anna's butterfly. A perfect gust of wind caught it, and she let out the string, watching the colorful kite soar until it grew smaller and smaller against the blue sky. Smugly, she called to Justin whose kite still wasn't up. "Need a hand there?"

He deliberately ignored her teasing and ran along the beach, Lamond at his side. Finally their kite caught an updraft and was swept into the air.

An hour of flying the kites wore out the adults, and they retired to the blanket under the umbrella. Mauli took the opportunity to head back to the hotel for a shower.

Justin reclined on the blanket with his hands stacked behind his head and his eyelids lowered.

From her comfortable canvas beach chair Meredith watched the boys run and laugh, calling to each another. When she turned and glanced at Anna, then Justin, she found him watching her. A dozen questions played in his deep chocolate eyes. But he hadn't asked any of them, giving her the freedom to relax with him, to be herself and to enjoy this time with no strings or expectations or judgments.

His friendship was a gift, offered freely.

"We don't know much about each other, do we?" she said softly, thinking out loud.

He smiled easily and shrugged.

"I was raised in the Midwest," she said. "Nebraska. My folks relocated to Portland when I was a teen."

"So you're a farm girl."

She rolled her eyes. "Why does everyone think all of Nebraska is overrun with cows and chickens? I happened to have lived in a city bigger than Portland."

He chuckled. "Excuse me, Miss Metropolitan."

She couldn't hold back a grin.

"I grew up in eastern Oregon," he told her. "Two older sisters and a younger brother."

"I'm an only child," she said.

He nodded and asked nothing.

A couple with three small children passed their umbrella, and Justin turned his attention to his boys for a few minutes.

His company was so comfortable, even silences

between them were companionable. She let out a contented sigh.

Turning back, he raised his eyebrows in a question.

She shrugged. "It's nothing really. Just that it's been a long time since I've relaxed and enjoyed myself like this."

A long moment passed, during which the surf roared and seagulls called overhead. "It's been a long time since I thought of myself as something other than a father or an attorney," he said at last. "Or half of a whole, left behind to sort through life." He nodded as though confirming what he'd just said. "That's it exactly."

She studied his expression, absorbed his words.

"I haven't felt like a man," he said finally, and she understood his feeling.

"I couldn't begin to know what it's like to lose someone the way you did."

"It's not real at first." He sat up and folded his forearms over his knees, staring out at the ocean. "There's a sort of cocoon of denial you wrap yourself in, because the situation is so surreal. But then you have to face the days and the nights. And other people…and your children. Pretty soon the truth won't stay at bay."

He glanced at her. "And when the truth does sink in, it's followed by anger and fear…and grief." His gaze returned to the surf and sky. "And to keep the grief from overwhelming you, it's right back to the denial. I'm okay, the kids are okay, all that. Pretty soon the denial becomes all there is."

"Maybe it's not as much denial as it is begrudging acceptance and determination to be okay," she suggested. "I see it in my young patients all the time. If they refuse to dwell on what they can't do and focus on what they can, it makes all the difference in their progress."

Justin moved his position to sit closer to her chair. When he reached up and took her hand, she held fast to his. "Maybe it's getting away," he said. "Maybe it's because enough time has passed…but I tend to believe it's because we met that I feel more hopeful about things, more optimistic about myself than I have for a long time. I'm looking past this moment and this single day of survival to something else."

She understood survival. She understood taking one day at a time. Her throat tightened with emotion. She could tell him about what she'd been through, but the words wouldn't form. The last man she'd spoken the word *cancer* to had split in record time, and that rejection wasn't an easy thing to forget.

Justin got to his knees and, still holding her hand, looked into her eyes. "This is going to sound really corny, but it's true. I haven't talked to anyone like this for a long time. I feel as if you get what I'm saying and you're not criticizing me for what I'm feeling.

Nor are you trying to dump a bunch of worthless plat-itudes on me. You don't expect me to cheer right up and forsake my coping mechanisms for what you think I should be doing."

His hand was warm and his eyes were filled with sincerity. The urge to say more rose inside her, but she knew she couldn't. She'd done too much coping herself to be critical of anyone else's methods.

"Is me spilling my guts making you uncomfort-able?"

She shook her head. "No."

"Good." He smiled at her then, and the tempting crease in his cheek drew her hand. She placed her fingers against his skin.

His smile faded and his dark, intent gaze bored into hers.

With a flutter of nervous anticipation, she raised her chin in invitation.

Justin closed the distance between them and pressed his lips against hers.

Eight

The kiss was warm and tentative, a gentle sampling of something they'd both been wondering about. She moved her fingers from his cheek to the back of his neck and tilted her head ever-so-slightly to deepen the contact.

Justin brought both hands up to cup her face, sliding his fingers into her hair behind her ears, moving his lips over hers in an increasing quest of discovery and sensual pleasure. Meredith's heart fluttered and, along with the sound of surf and seagulls, she could almost hear surprise and delight whoosh in her ears.

She relaxed and breathed, enjoying the measured

pressure of his lips, the feelings that brought her body and her heart to life, and the way he kissed her with respect and reverence and a touch of awe that made her ache inside.

Justin was the one to end the kiss, leaving her vaguely disappointed and out of breath.

He rested his forehead against hers and kept his fingers in her hair. "Was that too soon? Too much?"

With her eyes still closed, she let her hand trail from his neck to his shoulder. "Yes. No. I don't know. Probably."

"Was it okay?"

She nodded, moving his head with hers. "More than just okay."

He sat back, taking her hands in his, and she opened her eyes to see him, this stranger with the sexy smile and a heart-stopping look of purpose in his sparkling eyes.

"Since we've moved forward a little, do you think we could spend some time alone tonight? Will you have dinner with me?"

Her only hesitation was Anna.

"Mauli will keep Anna," he said intuitively. "She's completely trustworthy. Unless you have other misgivings."

"I have a lot of misgivings," she said, her mind racing, "but they're all about me. I want to have dinner with you."

One side of his lips turned up and he gave her fingers a gentle squeeze. "Okay."

Jonah called for his dad then, and releasing her hand, Justin went to join his boys.

Shortly after, Anna awoke and Meredith called to Justin. "I'm taking Anna in now. I'll see you a little later."

He waved. "I'll take care of the umbrella and chair for you."

Once inside, Anna nursed and stayed awake for quite a while. Meredith played with her, then wound the musical crib mobile to entertain the baby while she showered.

While she dressed and did her hair and makeup, she placed Anna nearby in her infant seat so she could talk to her. She chose a sleeveless dress she'd packed just in case and paired it with sandals, glad she'd painted her fingers and toes with the nail polish Chaney had given her. Bright red wouldn't have been Meredith's first choice, but it was fun and sexy and fit her cheerful mood.

Chaney had even slipped a silver ankle bracelet in the basket, and Meredith took it from its cardboard anchor and clasped it on.

She looked at herself in the full-length mirror on the closet door and pressed her fingers to her flushed cheeks. She hadn't taken this much care or been this eager since prom night in high school.

A vision of Veronica's disapproval if she knew about Meredith's date tonight flashed in her mind's eye and she immediately quashed the thought. Her mother was a disappointment she'd been forced to deal with time and again. She couldn't change Veronica, so she was learning to do what was best for herself without the woman's support or approval.

She coaxed Anna to nurse again, packed a bag with supplemental formula and a bottle and had just turned on her cell phone when Justin knocked at the door.

He wore a pair of dark green trousers and a sport jacket. The pullover shirt underneath was ivory colored and soft looking. At his handsome appearance, her breath locked in her chest.

His appreciative gaze returned her observation, touching on her hair, which she'd curled and left loose, then admiring her dress and bare legs. "I guess it's the real thing," he said.

"What do you mean?"

He grinned. "It must be a real date because we both dressed up."

She brushed her palms over her hips nervously and returned a hesitant smile. "I know. I haven't done this for a while, either."

"Well, since we're both out of practice, we'll get the hang of it together, how's that?"

He always set her at ease; it was one of the many

things she enjoyed about his company. She turned into the room and picked up her purse and Anna.

Justin gathered the infant seat and diaper bag. "The boys are looking forward to entertaining Anna for the evening."

"I've never left her before," she confessed. "I'm doubly nervous."

"I'll grab my phone," he said. "Mauli will call if she needs anything."

"Oh, I have mine," she replied. "I've written down my number, along with three pages of instructions and suggestions. She's going to think I'm obsessive."

He followed her out the door. "A mother is obsessive. It's her job. Got your key?"

She double-checked her purse for the plastic card. "Check."

They took an elevator to the second floor and Justin led her to a door where he used his key card. The elegantly appointed room was nearly identical to hers. The boys abandoned the video game they were playing to greet Meredith and Anna.

Mauli set Meredith at ease by listening to all her instructions and promising to call at the least problem.

"I've never left her before," Meredith said.

"No!" Mauli said with mock surprise and then gave her an understanding smile. "This is as good a time as any," she assured her, taking the baby.

"I don't know how she'll do with the bottle."

"If she won't take it, I'll call you."

"She should be good for a couple of hours anyway," Meredith said, kissing Anna's head. "Bye, sweetie."

Jonah and Lamond gave their dad hugs, and Meredith and Justin slipped out into the hall. Clutching her purse, she joined him in the elevator, and her stomach dipped as the car descended. "It feels really strange not to be carrying her."

When the elevator stopped and the doors slid open, Justin stood halfway out and used his back to prevent them from closing. "You sure you want to go? We can still change our minds and eat pizza with the kids."

She studied his face for thirty seconds. "I want to go. I have to leave her eventually. Pretty soon I'll be taking her to day care while I work. This is a good way to ease into the separation."

"I don't want you to be uneasy."

She stepped past him into the lobby. "I'm fine. Come on."

Daylight was waning as he held the passenger door of his Lexus for her and held her hand. She stepped up.

"I have a place in mind if it's okay with you," he said, getting in and starting the engine. "It's about a half-hour drive down the coast. Not too far in case Mauli should call."

"That's fine."

He took the state highway along the beach, past Oswald West State Park and on to a cape that held a cluster of buildings, among them The Blue Whale.

Once inside the dimly lit restaurant, they were seated near a wood-burning fireplace and with a view of the ocean. An oil lamp glowed at the side of their table, and the ambience was that of an eighteenth-century tavern, with the employees in period costume.

"I love this place," Meredith said after taking it all in. "How did you know about it?"

"It's in the tourist guide."

She glanced at the lamp. "Do you suppose that's whale oil?"

He grinned and picked up his menu. "I doubt it."

She, too, looked over the variety of dinners.

He surprised her by pulling out a pair of glasses and slipping them on to peruse the cuisine. "I suppose one must eat seafood when one is vacationing on the coast."

"One should," she replied, amused. She'd picked up on the fact that he spoke like an attorney when he got nervous. "I've never had such excellent fish as I've had during my stay here."

"What sounds good?" he asked.

"A steak."

He removed the glasses and chuckled. "I wasn't going to admit I've been craving beef the past two days."

"Well, now our secret is out."

"We could get the steak and lobster for two," he suggested. "That way we can say we had the local specialty."

"Excellent idea, Counselor."

He took her menu and laid them both aside. "I can't even impress you with my wine selection."

"You don't have to impress me. And please, order a glass. I'll take a tiny sip so I'll know what I'm missing. I promise I'll be impressed."

When the waitress returned, he ordered for them, and a few minutes later she brought his wine, followed by their salads and warm, crusty bread.

"Tell me more about the children's camp you want to start," he said.

"Well…I want to develop a nonprofit summer camp with modified boats and docks, special riding gear and the whole bit. I was able to raise small donations, but not enough for a lease on a campsite or the insurance. As I've mentioned before, I was working on bigger prospects when I—I had a personal setback."

Justin asked nothing. "Have you been able to move forward again?"

"Just barely. I devoted the last year to my pregnancy and to Anna. But I want to get back to seeking funds. Once I get enough money for the location and the medical equipment and all that, then I'll still need volunteers to staff the camp. It will take a host of professionals—nurses, doctors, therapists, nutritionists. Amazingly enough I've had people come to me and offer their time and expertise once the ball gets rolling."

"There are a lot of caring people in the world," he said. "More than we learn about, because the media plays up the negative aspects of society."

They talked more about her plans, and soon their meal was delivered.

They ate leisurely, conversing and occasionally watching the reflection of the moon on the ocean. Justin offered her a sip of his wine and she tasted it, finding it sweet and full-bodied.

He deliberately turned the stemware to the place where her lips had touched and drank. Warmth not caused by wine curled in her stomach, and she vividly recalled the feel of his lips on hers that afternoon. She wanted to experience the sensation again…and again.

His dark eyes sparkled in the glow of the lantern as he raked his gaze over her face and hair. "Before today I'd never touched anything as soft as your hair," he said, his voice a deep rumble.

She knew no reply, so she simply reveled in that knowledge and the headiness of being sexually appealing.

"Your hair's cute when you tie it up," he went on, "but I'm glad you wore it loose tonight. I like to watch it move and catch the light."

No man in her experience had ever been so attentive.

"Right now I'm wishing I could lean against you and bury my face in your hair," he said. "I'll bet it smells sexy."

Meredith took a sip from her stemmed water glass and her fingers trembled.

"Am I making you uncomfortable?"

Uncomfortable? As in her heart doing this staccato number in her chest? Warmth pooling in her belly and her breasts tingling? Oh, yeah. She shook her head, knowing the action would draw attention to the hair he admired. "You're making me…" *Hot.*

He raised one eyebrow.

"Feel attractive," she managed finally.

"You're more than attractive, Meredith. You're beautiful and sexy and intelligent." He paused and laced his fingers together, elbows on the table. "I'm sorry if I'm embarrassing you. I have this habit of saying what I'm thinking, and I've been doing a lot of thinking—all about you."

She glanced out at the ocean view and instinctively, self-protectively analyzed what was happening. "This is probably one of those vacation flings. We're away from our normal lives, relaxed and letting down our guard. Our paths crossed and we found something a little mysterious in each other."

"I don't know," he replied. "I've been on several

vacations since my wife died, but I've never seen a woman the way I'm seeing you. Nor have I had the thoughts I'm having."

What were those thoughts? Images of them together in an intimate tangle raised her temperature and caught her breath. His reflection came into focus on the window glass. Her skin warmed.

Meredith was a born optimist, always focusing on the positive, rarely giving in to despair or self-pity. But since the last man she'd believed cared about her had deserted her when she'd needed him the most, she'd been unable to trust again. Unable to even *think* of trying to develop another relationship.

She had learned the hard way that when push came to shove, there were only two people she could count on: Chaney and herself.

She wasn't a needy person.

But she was a woman.

A young woman with emotions and wants and physical desires…. It had been too long since she'd felt desirable.

"But I do find you exciting and a little mysterious," Justin added.

She turned her gaze from his reflection to the flesh-and-blood man. His eyes smoldered with desire, and she felt it all the way to her toes.

The waitress brought them one decadent chocolate-and-raspberry dessert, two forks and cups of steaming coffee—decaf as he'd requested.

They shared the dessert, and it melted on Meredith's tongue. Delicious, it was an indulgence she didn't often allow herself.

Like this time with Justin.

Like the kiss they'd shared that was still fresh in her memory.

Like her growing desire....

Nine

"Do you want to call?" Justin asked as they crossed the darkened parking lot.

She cast him a sheepish glance, loving that he'd asked. "You wouldn't mind?"

"Of course not."

They paused near the Lexus as she fished her phone from her purse and found the number she'd programmed in earlier.

Mauli answered.

"How's she doing?" Meredith asked.

"She's just fine. She was a little reluctant to take the bottle at first, but she got the hang of it and drank almost six ounces."

"Oh, my goodness." Meredith would have to pump if Anna had another feeding like that this evening. One hand went automatically to her breast, but she dropped it at Justin's notice of her action. She looked away. "Well, that's good, I guess. I don't hear anything in the background."

"The boys fell asleep watching a movie, and I've been playing with Anna. Her eyelids are looking heavy now."

"Try laying her down and leaving her alone. She's used to putting herself to sleep."

"Okay. Having a good time?"

"A great time." She turned and found him studying her in the darkness. Her heart took a little dip in her chest. "Justin found a fabulous place to eat."

"Tell me all about it later. If Anna falls asleep, I'm going to check my e-mail, and then I'll probably go to bed myself. I'll call if she wakes and has any problems."

"Thanks. You're a dear."

"Anna's the dear."

Meredith hung up and blinked away a few tears as Justin opened the door and she got into the SUV. She felt his curious gaze as he drove out of the parking lot. "She's doing just fine," she told him.

"And that makes you sad?"

A self-deprecating chuckle escaped her. "A little. I can't imagine what kindergarten will be like."

He laughed out loud. "What about college? And then, don't forget, she'll get married."

She waved at him. "Stop it."

He took her hand and held it snugly in his, resting it on the seat between them as he drove.

They'd gone a few miles before he found a stretch of beach and parked above it. Taking a jacket from the back of the vehicle, he draped it around her shoulders. The intoxicating scents of leather and man enveloped her, and they descended wooden stairs to the sand below.

Meredith was glad to feel his strong fingers close around hers again. They strolled along the beach, well away from the chilling cold spray of the surf. The sound was like the relaxation tape she'd used during her childbirth classes and labor. Chaney had been with her during those times. Meredith wondered what she'd tell her friend about this night and these developments.

Putting her feelings about Justin into words would be like trying to stop the ocean's tide with her bare hands.

Justin studied the lovely woman beside him in the moonlight. He felt out of his element with Meredith. Though she was obviously self-reliant and capable, he sensed an underlying vulnerability that kindled his protective instincts. Buying her meals and paying for their shared activities had been about as far as he'd dared go without compromising her independence.

She was right when she'd said they'd met under relaxed conditions. He definitely found her exciting and mysterious. He hadn't been with a woman for a long time. He hadn't known he would want to be. And he certainly hadn't expected to desire this particular woman.

Though she held a lot of herself in reserve, she seemed comfortable with him…and attracted to him. She neatly evaded subjects she didn't wish to discuss, such as her family and her baby's father. He could only assume the two were a bad combination. But she was more than happy to discuss her passions: Anna, her work and the camp she wanted to start. Those were the safe areas.

"You took on a big task," he said finally, "choosing to raise a child alone."

She nodded. "I wanted a child, and I was discouraged with the idea of needing a husband to make one. I figured I was doing okay by myself, how much more difficult could one little baby be?"

"More difficult than you imagined?"

She hesitated, as if considering her answer. "It's complicated."

"Because she's half-black."

Meredith looked at him. "I didn't realize what she'd need or want to know when she's older. What do I know about black heritage?"

"What if she was half-Italian? Or half-French? Would that seem so foreign to you?"

"Honestly? Probably not."

He appreciated her honesty, and expected nothing less from her. "So it's because of skin color."

"It is the visible difference. I was…intimidated."

"Has Mauli helped?"

She nodded. "Mauli has given me the encouragement I needed. She even offered to extend her friendship once we're back home. For someone so young, she has such wisdom and confidence. That's what I want for Anna."

"A lot of parents wouldn't recognize the importance of teaching their child about their heritage or bother to help them blend in. Anna is going to have all the skills she needs because you'll be equipping her."

They paused and studied the waves lapping against the sand. Here and there, rocks jutted from the constantly moving water.

"I'd be happy to help any way I can," he offered, drawing her gaze. "I take the boys to cultural events now and then. We could go together."

"Thank you," she said softly. "That means a lot to me." She turned to study the ocean. "Your friendship means a lot. And knowing that you don't want it to be temporary."

Meredith's pale profile was illuminated by the moonlight, and in that moment Justin recognized more than ever that her delicate beauty belied an inner strength he admired. Her fragility was a seductive deception, an age-old lure. The wind lifted her hair and blew strands across her cheek. "No, I don't want this to be temporary."

He raised his free hand to gently move away the tress. She looked up at him, and his breath caught in his chest. If he wasn't too out of practice and was reading all the signals right, she'd been affected by his words at dinner. And she wasn't immune to his nearness or his touch.

Releasing her hand, he used both of his to thread his fingers into the hair on each side of her face and run them through the cool length.

Her head dropped back and her eyes drifted closed.

The invitation too much to resist, Justin buried his hands against her scalp and leaned forward. When his lips met hers she made a breathy sound, part sigh, part sob that set him on fire.

She was a sensory overload for a man so long without female stimulation. Her lips were warm and pliant, and she tasted of coffee and chocolate.

She moved against him spontaneously. With both of their jackets opened, her full breasts pressed against his chest, she raised one arm to wrap it around his neck as though to secure the kiss for her lingering pleasure.

Her other hand flattened on his shirt, where he knew she could feel the beat of his thundering heart.

When they melded closer, he figured she recognized the most prominent part of his physical reaction. It felt so good to hold her, taste her, that he had to restrain himself from grinding his body against hers.

He lowered his hands from her hair to slide them inside the warmth of the jacket she wore, around to her back. She felt incredibly good, so feminine and soft, and he held her fast against him.

Quite naturally, without one or the other initiating it, their lips parted and the kiss deepened. She made that inciting little sound again, and this time he felt it against his tongue.

She pulled her mouth away, but bracketed his face between her hands so he wouldn't move. She kissed his chin, then his jaw, and the breeze chilled the trail of dampness.

Justin lowered his face to the lee of her neck and inhaled her intoxicating scent. She smelled like coffee everywhere; he'd probably get hard just driving past Starbucks for the rest of his life.

He was so hot that when she said, "My feet are cold," it took him a minute to register the fact and lead her back up the embankment to his vehicle. He held the door while she shook sand from her sandals, then once she was settled, he started the engine and turned on the heater.

"I'm sorry," he said. "I wasn't thinking how cool it gets out there at night."

"I shouldn't have worn sandals."

"Turn around and put your feet up here." He patted his lap.

She removed her sandals again and lifted her feet, using the jacket to cover her knees when her dress hiked upward.

Justin turned toward her, taking both of her feet in his lap to rub warmth into them, discovering as he did so that the soles were ticklish.

Touching her turned him on, and he ran his hands under the jacket, finding the delicate bracelet that circled her ankle. He skimmed his palms up her calves to the baby-smooth skin behind her knees. "You're soft everywhere," he said.

One of her bare feet had come in contact with his erection. "And you're not."

They laughed together, the intimacy releasing tension, creating a comfortable closeness. His desire was evident and she was well aware. And apparently she was okay with it, so the first few bridges had been crossed.

This was how it began. It had been so long for him that it felt like the first time he'd waded the shores of sexual discovery. In the darkness he heard her intake of breath when he reached under her dress and stroked the back of her thigh, then leaned forward to slide his hand to the curve of her buttock.

He came in contact with a silky undergarment and ran his fingers under the elastic.

Her foot pressed into his arousal. He couldn't reach her to kiss her, and the tension grew unbearable.

As though sensing his frustration, she withdrew her feet, moved them to the floor and slid closer. Justin immediately pulled her into his embrace and kissed her hard.

Her breathing was fast and shallow, and she pulled her mouth from his to catch her breath while she cupped his face in her palms and caressed the corners of his lips with her thumbs. One thumb rubbed across his damp lower lip, twice, three times before she plucked a kiss there.

Eager for more, Justin took her mouth in a possessive kiss, pressing her back against the seat and caressing her shoulders and back. She felt small and delicate beneath his hands, and the silken texture of her lips had him in a daze. He dropped his mouth to her neck, tasted the pulse point at her throat and lowered his hand to cover her breast through the fabric of her dress.

He sensed her discomfort then and paused.

"Maybe we should drive now," she said breathlessly.

Before things went too far? Or in order to get back to the hotel so they could continue? He waited for a clue, some indication of her desire.

"Okay," he said, pulling away and retrieving the

jacket from where it had fallen halfway to the floor. He handed it to her.

She threaded her fingers through her hair, straightened her skirt and fastened her seat belt.

Justin snapped his in place and ran a hand over his face before glancing in the rearview mirror and putting the vehicle in Reverse. Arousal, hot and needy, slugged through his veins. He reached for her hand, and she clasped his, drew it to her lips and pressed a moist kiss to his fingers.

When he turned to look at her, she smiled at him—a secret, sexy smile of want and expectation. A dozen erotic images flashed in his mind's eye.

It wasn't finished. It was only beginning.

Ten

Meredith's knees trembled as she and Justin entered the lobby, their fingers laced together. What was going to happen next? She knew what she'd like to have happen, what she thought they were leading up to… Her only hesitation was wondering how she could prevent Justin from seeing her breasts. How could she be with him and not get naked?

He looked at her, one brow raised in question. The moment drew out awkwardly. "I don't want you to be apprehensive," he said. "About me or about Anna. I don't want tonight to end, but I don't want to rush you."

"I don't want it to end, either," she admitted softly,

glancing around and making certain they were alone. "But I'd like to see Anna."

"All right. My kids and Mauli will be asleep." He led her toward the elevator and pushed the button.

"I could take her back to my room," she said. "And you could join me."

Desire burned in his expression. The doors opened and he gently tugged her forward. They stepped into the elevator and the doors swooshed shut. "Meredith, I don't want to push you into anything."

She leaned against him and their lips met in another exploratory kiss. "You're not pushing me," she breathed against his mouth. "I *want* this. I'm just a little…" She pulled away to say, "Self-conscious and…well, I'm not…perfect. I have some hang-ups."

"I don't want you to be uneasy with me," he told her. "Just let me know what you need and I'm there."

She didn't even know if she could express what she needed. At the moment, she needed to feel her baby in her arms, but he'd already acknowledged that.

The elevator stopped, and he led her to his room and opened the door. Inside it was dark except for a sliver of light coming from a crack where the bathroom door had been left ajar. Justin pointed to the adjoining suite. "That's Mauli's room. Tiptoe on in. I'll check on the boys."

Mauli was asleep in the bed, and beside her, sleeping soundly on her back on her own blanket was

Anna. Meredith gathered Anna's belongings and then touched Mauli's shoulder gently.

The girl roused and blinked at her. "Meredith?"

"Yes, I'm taking Anna with me now."

"Oh, okay. She was an angel."

"Justin is going to be with me a little longer, just in case you or the boys should need him."

"Okay."

"Night." By the time she picked up Anna, crossed the room and looked back, Mauli's eyes were closed again in slumber.

Justin led her out into the hallway. "The boys were sawing logs."

"I told Mauli you would be with me."

He nodded.

They took the elevator down, and this time Meredith spent the time gazing at her sleeping baby's relaxed face. She nuzzled Anna's hair and inhaled her familiar scent. "I'm going to try to wake her to nurse," she said.

"You getting uncomfortable?" he asked as they approached her door and he took the key from her.

Her cheeks warmed and she glanced up at him. "A bit."

He nodded his understanding and opened the door. He'd always been so easy with the fact that she breast-fed.

"You take all this in stride," she commented as they entered the suite. "Your wife nursed the boys?"

"Yes," he replied, flipping on a light in the sofa area. "Take your time. I'll watch CNN and catch up."

She carried Anna into the bedroom where she changed her diaper and left her on the bed while she slipped out of her dress. She roused her to nurse, and the whole time she thought about Justin and how this thing between them was going to progress. She wanted to make love with him, but she was afraid at the same time.

The sleepy baby contentedly dozed off and she placed her in the crib.

Meredith used the bathroom, brushed her hair and teeth and reapplied lipstick. Pausing to study herself in the mirror, she tried to calm her nerves. She was a mature woman, over thirty and in control of her life. She made decisions and choices for herself all the time. Justin was not a bad decision. She wanted him.

She needed the boost of confidence created by his desire for her. She needed to feel like a woman in the most basic way. She needed the human contact and the pleasure of intimacy.

A nursing bra was not sexy lingerie, she deduced. She removed it without looking at herself in the mirror and went to the bureau to find a silk camisole and slip it over her head. She stepped back into her dress and left her sandals on the bedroom floor.

The night-light left enough light for her to see

Anna if she needed to return. She left the bedroom door open and went to join Justin.

He was seated comfortably on the plush sofa, sipping something from a glass. She'd heard him out here earlier and had pictured him making a drink from the tiny courtesy bar. "Mixed a drink?"

He muted the television and held the drink toward her. "No, just a soda."

She took a sip and handed the glass back.

"She sleeping again?"

Meredith nodded. "Like an angel."

They smiled at each other and she felt the first awkward tension she'd ever experienced in his presence.

Justin ran his fingers up her arm, creating a delicious shiver. He set his glass aside and leaned to tug her onto his lap. She went eagerly, and he enfolded her in a welcome embrace.

"You feel so tense," he said against her hair.

"It's been a while."

"A year if I'm not mistaken," he said with a smile in his deep voice.

He would think that, since Anna was three months old, and a pregnancy took nine. But it had been a lot longer actually. He just had no way to know, because she hadn't told him. What was she afraid of? she wondered guiltily. Judgment? Having her choices analyzed?

He leaned to the side and switched off the table

lamp, leaving the flickering, muted television the only light.

He caressed her cheek, his touch cool from the glass he'd held. She reached up and traced his mobile lips with a fingertip. The yearning in her belly hadn't gone away, and it flamed to life now, fueled by the desire in his sparkling, dark eyes and the feel of his strong, hard body enveloping hers.

She sat up, a hand going to his shoulder. "Kiss me now."

"Yes, ma'am." His lips closed over hers, cool at first and then warming from the heated contact. Meredith touched her tongue to his lips and he parted them, taking the initiative to deepen the kiss. He tasted like the peppermint she'd seen him slip into his pocket after dinner.

Everything but that moment went out of her mind and she reveled in the sensory rush of feelings and delightful discoveries. He spanned her rib cage with both hands, slid his palms up until his thumbs rested under her breasts, coming in contact with her fullness through the fabric and sending a ripple of sensation across her flesh.

Her biggest apprehension stole some of the pleasure. She placed both hands over the backs of his, holding them in place so he wouldn't move them upward and discover her imperfection.

"Off limits?" he asked intuitively.

Embarrassment warmed her cheeks.

"It's okay," he said, and ran one hand down over her hip and stroked her bottom through her dress. "I can appreciate that part of you belongs just to Anna."

It wasn't that at all and she couldn't go on without telling him the truth. She stood and took a step backward, her heart racing.

"Meredith?"

She held a hand out for him to stay put and he did. "There's something I have to tell you."

"What's wrong?"

"Nothing's wrong. Just let me say it, okay?"

"Okay."

She inhaled and pursed her lips.

His expression remained calm, but then he was a lawyer, used to keeping his cool. Only one telltale muscle in his jaw gave away his apprehension.

"I had cancer," she said finally, the admission bringing a lunge to her midriff. But a swift tide of relief followed because she'd finally said the words it had taken her so long to form.

His expression showed he was plainly stunned. But he said nothing.

"Breast cancer," she explained. "I had two surgeries, followed by radiation. They got it all."

"Thank God" was all he said.

"That was two years ago. I have scars and some disfiguration where so much tissue was removed.

And my breast...." She touched her hand to the top of her right breast. "This one, doesn't produce as much milk, so it looks funny. I haven't... Well, I'm self-conscious about it."

And afraid. So afraid he wouldn't want her now that he knew. So afraid that he was another man who wouldn't be able to handle imperfection or difficulties, even though her logical mind told her he was not the same man as Sean.

"You told me there was a man who didn't stick around and you alluded to the fact that he couldn't deal with something."

She nodded.

"Was it the cancer he couldn't deal with?"

"I'd been diagnosed and had the surgery. The doctors were giving me my options regarding treatment. Some of the approaches were pretty scary. When a woman has to have chemo, they shut down her ovaries. We were terrified we'd never be able to have the children we both wanted." She swallowed hard.

"That was when the bastard split?"

"Yes. However, the doctors believed that they'd removed all the cancerous tissue and I opted for a less aggressive therapy. So I had six weeks of radiation."

"Who was there for you?" he asked, as though that was his only concern. "While you went through that?"

"Chaney. And my folks."

He sat forward and shook his head as though to clear it. "I had no idea."

"You wouldn't have."

He reached for her hand and kissed the backs of her fingers. "Thank you for telling me."

"I don't want you feeling sorry for me…." She wanted to say more, but Justin darted his tongue out and moistened her knuckles. He took her fingertip between his teeth and then closed his lips over it.

Sensation rocketed up her arm to pebble her breasts. He deliberately kept his gaze averted, drew her closer and pressed his face to her neck.

"Does it bother you that I don't want you to see me?" It was easier to ask when he wasn't looking at her face.

"No." His tongue dampened her skin and he gently bit the tendon in her neck. A shudder of sensation coursed through her frame. "I'm just grateful that you're healed. And alive."

Tears welled up and dampened her lashes. She closed her eyes.

"Is that it?" he asked. "All you had to tell me? You're not an escaped convict or a kidnapper or anything?"

She smiled through her tears and shook her head. "No."

"Good, you had me worried for a minute." With strong hands, he turned her around so that he could undo her dress. He slid the zipper down, the sound seeming to echo in the silence. He leaned to the edge of the sofa and raised the back of her camisole to press his lips against the small of her back. His warm breath dampened her skin and raised gooseflesh down the backs of her legs.

The dress fell to her ankles.

He bracketed her hips and she stepped out of the garment. His warm mouth found the skin of her back again and he ran his palms down her legs and back up, setting her on fire with each touch.

With gentle urging, he turned her to face him where he sat and pulled her forward, raising her camisole only enough to dart his tongue around her navel and along her waist.

She steadied herself with her fingertips on his shoulders, drowning in the sensations created by his gently arousing lips and hands.

Needing to return the caresses and touch more of him, she undid the few buttons on his shirt and bent to tug the hem upward. Justin helped her by pulling the shirt over his head.

Meredith's breath stopped. He was magnificent, with broad shoulders and muscled arms and chest. His sleek skin drew her to explore it, and her contrasting hand was pale and small against his flesh.

It seemed quite natural to move forward when he sat back, and she straddled his lap, running her hands over his shoulders and chest. He flattened his palms against her back and pulled her forward, his lips seeking hers. She lowered her head and kissed him, breathless now, a burning need pulsating low and heavy in her body.

He gripped her hips and pushed his upward, and through the flimsy barriers of fabric, she felt his arousal.

It was real, this thing they were doing, she realized in a daze of passion. They were both fully aroused and pressing for more. For the first time her brain formed the question she should have thought of a long time ago.

"Justin," she said, holding his head still.

He kneaded her buttocks and answered, "What?"

"What about— I don't— I mean I'm not taking any birth control."

"I have something," he said, easily lifting her when he raised up to reach into his rear pocket and withdraw his wallet.

Thank God *he'd* been thinking straight. Grateful, she kissed him.

He ran his palms over her thighs, fingered the edge of her panties teasingly. Touching her then, through the damp fabric, he found her most sensitive spot. She moaned against his lips, encouraging his deft ministrations.

It wasn't enough anymore. She wanted to feel his skin against hers, wanted to have him filling her. "Where?" she asked on a ragged breath.

"Your bed," he said. "Or right here."

"Here?"

He nodded and nuzzled the sensitive flesh of her neck, then nipped a path to her chin.

"How?"

He ground her against his erection. "Just like this, baby."

"Ohh." The sensation and the image in her head turned her insides to liquid. His mouth on her throat had her body clamoring for more.

She stood again and he whisked her underwear down her legs and off. While she watched, he unfastened his pants and slid them and his boxers off into a pile. Her heart slammed against her chest at the sight of him. He was perfection: lean thighs, slender hips, a flat belly—and he wanted her. She reached out to touch him and he jerked at the contact, sucked in a breath and closed his eyes.

"You are perfect," she said, admiring his sleekly sculpted body.

He looked at her then, touched her hair with a tenderness and awe that brought more tears to her eyes. "You're beautiful, Meredith. Feminine and delicate. No woman has had this effect on me in years. I feel…so lucky to be here with you."

She smiled then. She was the lucky one. Two years ago she hadn't even known if she would be alive at this moment. And now here she was—alive, the mother of a beautiful baby girl and in the arms of a caring, honorable, sexy man. A laugh of pure joy rose up and tumbled out.

He enveloped her in a bone-crushing hug, kissing her senseless.

"Now, Justin," she said when she could breathe.

Eleven

It seemed she had waited a lifetime for this perfect moment. For this man who set her on fire, and at the same time he gave her the sense of peace and acceptance that she so desperately needed.

What could have been awkward was one of the most erotic things Meredith had ever done, and by the time Justin was sheathed, her fingers were trembling. He kissed her tenderly and asked, "Nervous?"

"A little."

He touched her again and she groaned against his temple. With little urging, she straddled him and lowered herself, her body quivering with anticipation.

With his face buried against her throat, he spoke

encouragement in that sensual, velvet voice. "You are so fine," he said, gripping her hips as she took her own time accommodating him. When he was buried inside her, they both released a sigh of pleasure.

He allowed her to discover her preferences, stroking her waist, her shoulders and thighs all while he told her how much she turned him on.

Tension built and Meredith grew focused, her breath shallow, her eyes closed. Her legs tired and he helped her, his strong hands and arms taking over the pace. Time stood still for an eternal, nerve-splitting moment. She didn't breathe.

In a blinding rush of pleasure and release, she gasped, the sound a series of staccato inhalations, ending with a release of breath and a sob.

Taking his own fulfillment quickly, Justin crushed her against him and buried his face in her hair.

It was a few minutes before either of them could move. When she raised her head, he lifted her gently away and stood, pulling her to her feet, then bent to pick her up with one of his arms behind her back and the other under her knees. She'd seen it done in dozens of movies and thought it was a delightfully romantic act.

Carrying her into the bedroom, he set her down so he could turn back the covers, then placed her in the middle of the bed and joined her. "This is the place for cuddling."

She nestled against him, her head automatically resting on his chest and her hand lazily stroking his belly. "That was…." She could tell he was waiting. "Intense."

He chuckled. "Indeed."

He held her, stroking her back through the silk camisole she still wore.

Justin's chest was tight with emotion he'd never expected to feel. Meredith was a strong, sensitive woman, beautiful and courageous and sexy as hell. Any man who could desert her so unfeelingly when she'd needed him wasn't worth the tears she had undoubtedly cried.

After what she'd been through, Justin understood her hesitancy to tell him, appreciated her fear of being vulnerable. And he understood her decision to have a child alone. After a man had done that to her, she'd probably figured she was better off without one. But it made him curious about Anna's parentage. If her ex-fiancé wasn't Anna's father, that meant she'd been with another man and had chosen to have his baby alone. Did the man even know he was a father?

Justin had already considered that he didn't need any complications in his life. He had enough going on with his kids and his job. What if something came up in the future? What if the guy suddenly wanted to be a father or see his child?

But Meredith wasn't a complication. She wasn't a threat to his family or his life that he could see.

He was enamored with her, and maybe it was just sex, but he didn't think so. He'd started out wanting to be her friend and ended up as her lover. And he didn't want it to be only for their brief time at Cannon Beach. There was the possibility of something good here; he felt it.

She'd trusted him with her insecurities. She'd opened herself up to physical and emotional intimacy, and he understood what courage that had taken. She was an enigmatic combination of strength and fragility, and she turned him inside out with desire.

Already he felt himself growing hard against her thigh.

She stroked his cheek and ran a finger over his lips, tugging the lower one playfully, then turned her face up to his for a kiss.

Justin raised on his elbow to stroke her slender hip and the length of her long silky thigh and calf. Her skin was pale and delicate, a pleasing and erotic contrast to his. He hooked her behind the knee and pulled her leg over his hip.

She wrapped her free arm around his neck and he kissed her in a slow, deliberate act of seduction and arousal. Her responsive kisses were gentle and imaginative. She made feminine, kittenish sounds that nearly hurt him, they were so titillating.

When she touched him he groaned, a response dredged from his very sum and substance, and she greedily took his weight and held him fast with surprisingly strong limbs.

"Justin, do you have another—"

He untangled himself and hurried to find his wallet and returned to find her smiling, her silky hair in tangles, a glow of anticipation in her eyes. Even in the semidarkness he could see that her sweet lips were damp and swollen.

He deliberately pushed her to her back and pressed his face to the soft skin of her belly. He nudged her little camisole up just enough to taste the underside of her breast. She didn't stop him so he did the same to the other, then laved his way to her nipple and took it into his mouth.

She sucked in a breath and held it until he kissed his way back to her navel.

He sat and met her gaze with a smile he hoped showed her how he felt about her, about what they were doing. "You are so sexy," he told her.

"Yeah?"

"Oh, yeah."

She reached for him and he gritted his teeth against the intense pleasure. In minutes he was stretched out beside her again, kissing her, discovering ways to touch her that had her making those sounds that nearly pushed him over the edge. He'd never known a more responsive woman, and her pleasure became his sole purpose.

Somewhere in the dim recesses of his brain he knew there were other things he needed, like air, but none of that mattered now. Meredith was the center of his universe, and his passion and fulfillment re-volved around hers.

She climaxed under his touch as he watched her face and held her gaze. He kissed her tenderly and a single tear appeared at the corner of her eye. He touched a fingertip to it in amazement.

She placed her hand alongside his jaw, a touch that was as adoring and intimate as any she'd given him. She made him feel powerful and competent. He hadn't felt that way outside a courtroom for a long time. "It's not too soon?" he asked.

Her reply was to tighten her hold and urge him above her.

He lowered his weight, eased himself inside her and shuddered with the sheer pleasure of being one with Meredith.

"I can't get enough of you," he said, his voice gruff with desire.

She framed his face and kissed him as though she felt the same.

Tension intensified. Her body trembled and she strained against him. Justin steeled himself and held on until she gripped his shoulders and cried out, and then he relinquished control.

He rolled to his back and she snuggled against him, her fragrant hair soft against his neck, her cheek light against his shoulder. She fit alongside him as though she'd been made for him.

He liked that she didn't pretend or put on airs. Meredith hadn't minded letting him know when she was turned on and had returned his passion without hesitation. She was an incredible woman, and he was a little in awe of his good fortune in finding her.

"That was amazing," she said softly.

"You took the words right out of my mouth," he replied, a little apprehensive of something so good. He didn't want to acknowledge how remarkable this thing between them was because it had happened so quickly and still seemed so new and tentative.

On the other hand, he was a man who spoke his mind and he didn't want her to doubt that he wanted more than this one night or even the rest of their vacation time.

"It probably isn't fashionable to blurt one's feelings," he began.

"Fashionable?"

"It's uncool."

"What one feels doesn't have to be cool if it's honest," she said.

"Why do I think you're mocking me?"

She smiled against his cheek. "Continue, Counselor."

"We've found something good here," he said. "I don't want it to end when we go back to Portland."

She raised her head and looked at him, her hair a

tangle over one cheek, her hazel eyes a tawny brown in the darkness. "It was good," she agreed hesitantly.

He sat up quickly, taking her with him until they sat facing each other. "Not just the sex," he added, realizing how she must have taken his words. "That was great, fantastic. But I mean the connection we have here."

She smiled her understanding then. "I don't want that to end, either."

"We can work around our families," he said. "And with them."

"Okay."

"And jobs, too," he added. "We both have demanding careers. But it's possible. Right?"

"Yes."

Justin sounded so hopeful, so positive that Meredith allowed herself to believe it could be the way he said. He was a sincere and forthright person. If he said they would make it work, then they would. There was nothing she needed or wanted more at this point.

He extended a finger and ran it across her collarbone, gazed into her eyes. "You're beautiful, Meredith."

The nagging thought of the controversy her relationship with Justin would cause her family dimmed her joy. Her mother was incapable of accepting her right to her own life or her own choices. It had grown more and more apparent that Meredith would have to cut her ties in order to keep her sanity and her self-respect. The fact would slice her to ribbons inside if she didn't let it go, if she didn't acknowledge that her mother's attitude wasn't her fault or responsibility.

In all likelihood the woman would never approve. If Veronica found Anna—a sweet, precious, innocent baby—intolerable, a full-grown African-American male would be her undoing. As much as it hurt, Meredith had to get past expecting her mother's favor.

She clung to the knowledge that Chaney would be happy for her and her father would be accepting.

Meredith would have to tell Justin about her mother's prejudice. But there was time for that. For now the rest of the world was on hold—and best left that way.

Life would intrude soon enough.

Justin was awakened by the boys wrestling on the other side of his bed the following morning. He cracked open an eye and peered at the clock, then at the two of them. No wonder they were awake and raring to go; it was nearly nine. He hadn't slept this late in eons.

Wearing Spider-Man pajamas, Lamond bounced on the mattress. "Take this, you evil warlord," he said in a childishly deep imitation of a cartoon hero. He lunged toward Jonah, and the tussling duo landed on Justin's belly.

"Oomph!" He shot up, snaring them both around the shoulders and dragging them back against his chest where he squeezed them.

Squeals and cries erupted and another fight ensued.

Two energetic boys were more than an adequate match for a man exhausted from a night of physical activity and little sleep, so he surrendered and let them bury him under a mound of pillows and blankets.

Eventually he pushed himself up and stumbled toward the bathroom in his boxers. "I'm going to shower. Try to defeat the enemy quietly until I get back."

"What are we gonna do today, Dad?" Jonah called.

"We'll figure that out after I've had a cup of coffee."

After a refreshing shower and his first cup of coffee, his mind had cleared and he discussed options for the day with his sons. They had just decided on activities when his cell phone rang.

Justin picked up the phone from the night table, absently thinking he needed to charge it, and noted Terrence Logan's office number on the caller ID. Business. "Justin Weber," he answered automatically, thinking it was Terrence's secretary.

"Hello, Justin," Terrence said. "Is your vacation going well?"

An erotic vision of the previous night immediately registered in his sluggish brain. "Extremely well, thanks. How are things in Portland?"

"We've got some problems."

Justin's instincts were alerted. "What problems?"

"There's a situation here." He explained that a

nurse's suspicions had proven valid and that the FBI had been called in to investigate a black-market baby ring operating out of Portland General and Children's Connection.

Stunned, Justin absorbed the information, his mind already working over ways to keep the media out of it. "Don't talk to the investigators without me present," he told his longtime friend. "They can reach me at this number if they need a contact person. And don't let anyone say a word outside that room. I'll handle the press releases."

"There's probably nothing that can't wait until you're back," Terrence assured him. "I told the board you'd already postponed your vacation once and that I didn't expect you to cut it short."

"Thanks. I can probably start the ball rolling from here and follow up when I get back. Don't worry about it. I'll handle everything."

Silence ensued for a tense moment. Justin's sensors went on alert.

"That's not all," Terrence said finally, regret lacing his tone.

"What else?"

"It's the situation with the Malone woman. The board is pressing for some concrete decisions."

Justin recalled the reference to a clinic case he'd glanced at and passed over to his assistant to research. "We held off to give her privacy," Justin said. "At the time I thwarted the press. Has something leaked since?"

"No. But the board is insisting that you meet with her and her attorney and work out a settlement if there's going to be one."

"I can do that as soon as I get back."

"Maybe you can do it even sooner."

"What do you mean? Something like that can't be done over the phone."

"No, it can't." Terrence paused again and Justin got an uncomfortable knot in his stomach. It wasn't like Terrence Logan to be cryptic. "It was suggested that we offer her some time away to think and bond with her baby."

Justin was listening. In the background the boys had turned on the television and battle sounds erupted. "I guess that couldn't hurt."

"Well, it's done. The chairwoman offered her a suite for a couple of weeks."

A nagging discomfort crept along Justin's spine and his face felt numb. "When was this?"

"Last week. She's there now."

"There where?"

"At the inn."

Twelve

The horrible realization caught him full force. "Malone." He'd always heard the case referred to as "the Malone woman." "What's her first name?"

Papers rustled on the other end of the line. "Meredith."

Justin's scalp prickled. Dread engulfed his senses. How stupid could he have been? A white woman inseminated with the wrong sperm. A young woman with a half-black baby.

"Could you talk to her, Justin?"

Talk to her.

Talk to her?

Talk to her! Oh, he'd done more than talk to Meredith Malone.

"There's a fear here that she's going to sue the clinic and expose the error," Terrence continued. "That, combined with this kidnapping thing, could ruin us."

She'd sue for a hell of a lot more than a sperm mix-up if she thought Justin had come on to her with an ulterior motive. Talk about a conflict of interests! "I'm not in a good position here, buddy," he said when he found his voice. He gripped the back of his neck in a gesture of frustration and felt the tension knotting his muscles. "Holy— This is *not* good."

"What's wrong?"

"What's wrong?" He clenched his fist and struck the side of his palm against the window casing.

"Justin?"

His memory rolled back over Meredith's reactions to people looking at them in restaurants. She'd never had the African-American lover he'd imagined. She'd come by her mixed-race baby by accident. An accident made by a clinic for which he was legal counsel. How could he have never registered her first name?

Was he so busy and legal-minded that the people involved in his workload were merely case numbers and statistics? *The Malone woman.* A problem that needed taking care of.

The Malone woman. A soft, vulnerable, courageous person who had survived breast cancer, as well as a man dumping her. "She had breast cancer," he said aloud.

Paper rustled again. "That's not in this file. Her medical records are private anyway, so how did you know?"

"Her fiancé dumped her."

"Oh."

"She chose to have the child on her own."

"You know a lot about her."

"Apparently not enough."

"Justin, what's wrong? Have you seen her there? Can you talk to her?"

"Oh, I'm going to be doing a lot of talking," he replied.

"I'm getting the impression that you've already met her and you don't want to do this. Tell me I'm wrong."

Justin opened his mouth and shut it quickly. Panic rose in his chest and his heart raced.

Terrence said something under his breath, but Justin made out the curse word he himself had been biting back because his kids were within earshot. Anger rose up. The board had known that the two of them would come in contact at the inn.

"You helped set this up?" he asked.

"I didn't stop it," Terrence admitted. "The board was gung ho on the plan, and I guess I figured no harm could come if the two of you ran into each other. I'm sorry, Justin, because now it seems underhanded."

"I can't talk about this right now," Justin said finally. "I'm going to need some time to think."

"Keep in mind that the board's restless. They want this thing confronted and settled."

"Of course I want what's best for the clinic," he said. "But this is my *life* being screwed with."

"You'll get back to me."

"Yes." Justin turned off his phone and stared out the window at the gray morning fog over the ocean. The coffee in his belly had turned to acid and burned like fire.

Terrence Logan had been his friend for years.

He'd just met Meredith Malone.

The Children's Connection was his source of income and his number-one priority. It provided a hell of a living for his family.

She was in his blood. God help him.

There was no reason on earth that Mauli or Jonah or Lamond would understand not including Meredith in their plans for the day. There was no reason Meredith would understand either. So it was with dread and guilt that Justin picked up the phone and called her room.

"Good morning," she replied, and her voice stirred up memories of heated kisses and entwined limbs.

"Morning," he greeted her.

"Did you sleep well?" she asked with a smile in her voice.

"What little I slept."

"I know of a good herbalist if you're having trouble sleeping. She'll suggest something helpful."

Her teasing made him feel worse, but he didn't want her to think he wasn't every bit as interested today as he'd been the night before. "I think the only thing she could suggest would be that I stay in my own room."

"How much fun would that be?"

He closed his eyes and pictured her. The image hurt. "How does the wax museum sound? The boys want to see it. And there's still an operating lighthouse I want to check out. Then tonight I thought we could have a campfire on the beach."

"Sounds great."

"I don't want to monopolize all your time if you have shopping you want to do or just need time alone."

"I'd be pleased to join you, and I appreciate you including me."

"Good. About forty-five minutes okay?"

"I'll be in the lobby."

Meredith hung up and glanced outdoors where the sky and the beach looked cool and gray. She dressed accordingly in slim jeans and got out her denim jacket. She fed Anna and dressed her in a one-piece outfit with feet and long sleeves. She packed her bag, brushed out her hair, leaving it loose, and carried Anna to the lobby.

The boys rushed up to greet her and Meredith

lowered the baby so they could talk to her. Anna had a broad toothless smile for her new friends.

Justin stood to the side and she met his eyes. He gave her a smile and her insides jumped. She had it bad for this guy.

When neither she nor Justin moved, Mauli took the initiative to lead the small gathering out of doors.

The wax museum was a half-hour drive, and Mauli entertained the boys with a traveling game of I Spy. Meredith wished she had the freedom to scoot closer to Justin, lean against him or just touch him. She was an admittedly insecure creature and wanted to reassure herself that they were okay.

As though he understood or felt the same, he rested his hand between them on the seat and glanced at her.

When she reached over, he clasped her hand in his strong, warm grip, a touch that confirmed his feelings for her without words. A couple of times she caught him looking at her with an unexplainable look of concern, but then he'd say or do something to make her think she'd imagined it.

The farther they drove from the beach, the brighter the sky became. Before they got out of the SUV, Justin grabbed a camera and hung the strap around his neck.

The boys were delighted with the contemporary figures in wax. Mauli liked the presidents, and Justin took Meredith's picture with Anna and Elvis. He bought a fistful of postcards and in the car Mauli helped the boys write notes to their grandparents.

"Want one?" he asked her. "There are stamps in my planner."

She accepted the glossy picture of John Wayne and turned it over. She should send a card to her folks so that her dad would know she'd thought of him, but she wasn't due home for another week and she didn't want Veronica to know her whereabouts before then.

Instead she scribbled a note to Chaney. She would probably talk to her later today. What would she tell her friend about her situation? They were always open with each other. She didn't have anything to hide, but Justin was so new and their relationship so delectably fresh that she wanted to keep him to herself just a little longer. Was that foolish?

The sky and the ocean were painfully bright now that the fog had lifted. They removed their jackets and donned their sunglasses. Justin stopped at a lighthouse and they took a tour, then found an old-time soda fountain for lunch. Meredith insisted on paying for their meals, and he begrudgingly accepted.

She sat in the vehicle and fed Anna while the rest of them walked along a pier and investigated a few shops. When they returned, Lamond gleefully handed her a small square box with a silver sticker indicating the shop's name on top. "We got ya somethin'."

She looked at it with surprise. "A gift for me?"

Jonah stood beside his brother in the opening of the car door. "Dad says it's good for us to be generous and not always want stuff for ourselves."

"Well, that's true," she said, lifting the lid with a smile. Inside on a bed of velvet was a bracelet of ocean-blue stone and sterling-silver beads with a dangling heart at the clasp. She'd seen similar handmade jewelry in many of the shops and knew the pieces didn't come cheap.

Mauli had come up to stand beside the boys, and Justin towered over them. "Let me help you put it on," Mauli said.

While the nanny worked the clasp, Meredith met Justin's eyes and for the briefest moment thought she recognized anxiety. But then he gave her a lopsided and uncertain smile as though wondering how she was receiving the offering. Too much too soon? she wondered, then scoffed at herself, considering what they'd already shared.

She looked at the stunning bracelet on her wrist, then at the family waiting for her reaction. "It's the very one I would have selected for myself," she said earnestly. "It's lovely and it means a lot to me that you chose it for me."

"We picked it out together," Lamond said proudly.

"Thank you."

The boys grinned, Mauli glanced up at her employer and Justin simply nodded and ushered his boys into the vehicle.

Meredith handed Anna back to Mauli, who got her situated in her seat, and the afternoon was back under way.

"I need a couple of hours' rest," Justin admitted as they neared the inn. "Will you meet us on the beach around six?"

"Sure."

"We'll build a fire and have food, so bring your appetite."

"Not a problem."

Mauli led the boys across the lobby and out of sight. Justin, who had been carrying Anna, handed the infant to her mother. "I'll see you shortly."

She nodded and their gazes locked. She involuntarily dropped her gaze to his lips. He glanced over her shoulder. Then without further hesitation he bent and pressed a kiss on her mouth.

Thirteen

Meredith strolled to her room and let herself in, dropping her things on the nearby sofa and placing Anna in the crib to stretch out and entertain herself for a while. After her confinement in the car seat Anna seemed to like the freedom to kick and gurgled happily.

When her phone rang, Meredith answered it to hear her family-planning counselor's voice. "The paperwork substantiates that your eggs were used, Meredith. Of course there is one positive proof if you want it."

"DNA testing?"

"Exactly."

"I do," Meredith answered without hesitation.

"No problem. You and Anna can stop in at the clinic and we'll have a kit ready."

"That will be my first priority when we get home."

"Great. See you then."

Meredith hung up and dialed Chaney's cell phone.

"How's the weather?" her friend answered.

"Lovely."

"How's the tall nine-and-a-half with the brown eyes?"

Meredith couldn't hold back her enthusiasm. "He's incredible."

"As in a good date? A scintillating conversationalist? Or phenomenal in the sack?"

Meredith laughed. "All of the above, actually."

"Shut *up!* You didn't!"

"God, Chaney, I feel something with him that is just so right."

"You've never had sex with a guy without first analyzing the relationship and checking the alignment of the stars, so it must be more than right."

"You're exaggerating."

"Not much. This is unheard of."

"Yeah, well, I surprised myself."

"You shocked the crap out of me. Though I did tell you to enjoy yourself, didn't I?" Chaney chuckled. "What's this guy got that none of the others have had?"

"Class."

"Well, I'm jealous. When do I get to meet him so I can really feel bad?"

"I'll introduce you as soon as we get back to Portland."

"Does he have a friend? A brother? A cousin?"

"I don't know."

"How about a reasonably fastidious acquaintance?"

Meredith laughed. "I do have to tell you something that I haven't mentioned."

Chaney groaned. "He's *not* married! Don't you dare tell me you've mixed yourself up with an unobtainable man."

"No, of course not."

"Well, he sure isn't gay."

"No."

"What, then? He lives with his parents and his mother does his laundry?"

"No, I told you he's a widow with his own kids."

"I can't think of anything else that would keep him out of the running for Mr. Right, then. Surprise me."

"He's black."

Silence strained across the miles. Meredith waited with growing trepidation. "Chaney?"

"You did just say he's black."

"African-American."

"Well." A snort sounded over the receiver. "You surprised me, all right. Now I'm picturing you doing the horizontal mambo with Denzel Washington. Tell me, it *is* Denzel I should be imagining and not Chris Rock."

Meredith burst out laughing.

"Oh, my God," Chaney said, obviously sobering.

"What? No, no, Denzel is an excellent comparison."

"I'm beyond that, Mer. Now I'm seeing your mother when she finds out."

Immediately serious, Meredith sat on a chair that faced the window and studied the cloudless sky. "This will do it," she said, the regret a familiar weight on her heart. "This will dash any flimsy hopes I had of preserving a relationship with her."

"I'm afraid you're right. As if Anna wasn't enough."

"I came here to think things through, and I've been able to do that. If she can't accept Anna and my choices, then I can't have a relationship with her. It's a tough decision, but it's the only one I can make." Just saying the words hurt.

"I'm sorry, Mer. I didn't hold out much hope that she'd ever come around. You'll still have your dad. If she lets him see you."

"I'll have to see how that irons out," Meredith replied. "Hey."

"What?"

"Thanks for being my friend."

"Ditto, girlfriend."

"Talk to you soon."

"Guess I don't have to tell you to have fun."

"Guess not."

They said their goodbyes and Meredith cut the connection. If only her mother was a fraction as loving and accepting as Chaney.... She caught herself and corrected her thinking. She wasn't responsible for her mother's choices or reactions, though they hurt. She was entirely grateful for a wonderful friend.

And a perfect and healthy daughter.

And a budding new relationship.

Things looked better to her than they had for a long time.

The sunset that evening was a streaked palette of orange and lavender hues reflected on the water. They walked the beach, an obstacle course of rock and sea oats and grass, and the boys collected driftwood and shells. Screaming seagulls wheeled overhead, looking for a handout then disappeared into the deepening dusk.

Meredith, Mauli and the boys gathered wood and dried seaweed, and Justin started a fire. With a pocketknife he shaped sticks onto which they speared hot dogs and the adults helped the boys hold them over the fire. After they'd all eaten their fill, Jonah and Lamond sang every song they could think of, and then Mauli and Meredith took over with "The Farmer in the Dell" and "Old MacDonald."

Anna had been fed and Justin held her with her back against his chest and her bottom on his lap so she could watch the others. She was dressed in her pink-and-white hooded fleece jacket and pants, looking warm and adorable.

"Did we do this when Mama was with us?" Lamond asked during a break in the songs.

"We never came here," Justin replied.

"Did we sing on the beach in Florida?" he persisted.

"No, but we went for walks."

"Was I a little baby like Anna?"

Justin nodded. "Yes."

"Grandma says Mama loved to ski and so that's where you went on vacations."

"We went to the mountains a couple of times before Jonah was born," he said.

"Do you like to ski, Meredith?" Lamond asked.

"I've never been skiing," she replied.

"For a Florida native, your mom sure liked the snow and cold in the mountains," Justin told the boys.

"Did she sing songs?" Lamond asked.

Jonah didn't ask many questions, but he always seemed interested in hearing the answers to Lamond's. He looked to his dad for a reply.

Justin looked at his sons with pain revealed in his eyes. "Sure she did."

"You pick a song now, Dad," Jonah suggested.

Justin glanced down at Anna in his lap. "Okay. What

would you like to hear, Anna?" He raised her up and pretended she was saying something in his ear. "Good choice!" He lowered her back to her sitting position and launched into "I Heard It through the Grapevine."

After laughing with surprise, Meredith and Mauli piped in as his accompaniment, and the boys got up and danced around the campfire. The women hopped up and joined in. Their voices rang across the water and firelight flickered on each face.

Anna's eyes were wide and she stared from one person to the next in a way that made Meredith laugh so hard she couldn't sing. She collapsed to her knees.

"You're ruining our act here," Justin playfully chastised. "We might as well move on to the surprise."

"What's the surprise?" Jonah asked, and he and Lamond dropped beside him on the blanket.

Justin handed Anna to Mauli and opened a cardboard box he'd stashed earlier. He withdrew marshmallows, graham crackers and chocolate bars, eliciting cheers of appreciation for the upcoming s'mores.

Meredith speared marshmallows and instructed the boys on how to hold them over the flames. Justin prepared the graham crackers and broke the chocolate bars into pieces. In no time even the adults had sticky fingers and chocolate on their chins.

"You are *such* a bad influence," Meredith scolded at the same time she chewed and swallowed with blissful enjoyment.

"You knew I was a bad boy from the beginning," he said, licking his fingers.

She'd never had as much fun with anyone as she had with this man. And with his family. She was susceptible to his charm and his unique brand of warm humor. Seeing him with his children had touched her from the moment they'd met and seeing him with Anna brought stinging tears of joy to her eyes. When he spoke of his wife, she felt his loss and admired his strength.

He'd had an enormous influence on her in a short time, but it definitely wasn't a bad one, as she liked to tease.

Besides the incredible physical attraction and compatibility, there was more. Last night when he'd told her he wanted their relationship to continue, his openness and honesty had revealed even more about the man.

It was a scary thing to share feelings like that. It made a person vulnerable, but he had shared them anyway. She admired him for that and for so many things.

She was definitely smitten.

It grew late and the fire died down. "I guess it's time to get the kids in," Justin said.

"I can take them in, Anna, too, if you two want to stay awhile longer," Mauli offered.

"You're sure you don't mind?" Meredith asked.

"Not at all."

"I'll carry her in and get you a few diapers," she said, getting to her feet.

Justin stood and brushed off the knees of his jeans. "I'll add another log to the fire."

Meredith followed Mauli and the boys inside. Mauli herded them into the shower to rid themselves of sand and get ready for bed. "Got your phone?" she asked.

Meredith tapped her jacket pocket.

"I'll call if she gets hungry."

Meredith removed Anna's outerwear, kissed her head and turned her over to Mauli with a little wave as she returned to the beach.

Justin had stoked the fire while he waited and now handed Meredith a bottle of water as she sat down beside him. She unscrewed the cap and took a drink.

A sick feeling had plagued him all day and intensified as night drew closer. He didn't want to tell her who he worked for.

He couldn't stand deceiving her.

He didn't want to ruin the tentative relationship they'd formed.

And it was really unfair that he knew something she'd chosen not to share.

He had to tell her.

He pushed marshmallows on a stick. "Can you eat another one?"

She accepted the branch and held it over the flame. "I told Chaney," she said.

He looked up from the graham cracker he was breaking. "What did you tell her?"

"About us. I couldn't hold it back. I thought I wanted to savor it for a while, but then when I talked to her, it just came bubbling out."

The excitement in her voice was difficult to hear, knowing he was going to hurt her. "What did she say?"

"You'd have to meet Chaney to understand her comments." She glanced up at him. "She's happy for me. I think Mauli's caught on, too."

"She's giving us time together deliberately," he replied and placed chocolate on the graham cracker.

"Justin," she began, "my heart just goes out to your boys when they ask about their mother."

"I know," he said, his throat thick with emotion.

"And for you. Not only did you lose her, but you have to see what missing a mother is like for your children. You're so good with them. I admire you for the kind of parent you are. I mean, you have a high-pressure career and you're a hands-on dad at the same time."

"I just live one day at a time, Meredith, I don't think I deserve admiration for simply surviving."

"Don't sell yourself short," she said emphatically. "Sometimes surviving is everything."

"I'm sorry," he added, realizing what he'd thoughtlessly said. "You're right, of course."

"Damn right I am." She pulled the marshmallows away from the fire and let Justin slide them off and make their s'mores.

She got up on her knees so she was higher than him and looked into his eyes. "Did you mean everything you said last night?"

His heart lurched. "I did."

Behind him the waves lapped against the beach in a timeless rhythm.

"Still think I'm sexy?"

He hooked one arm around her waist and pulled her snugly against him. "Sexy doesn't even begin to cover it."

He fed her a bite, catching a string of melted confection and then licking his finger. They finished off the treat and she smiled disarmingly.

He had to tell her, but first he had to make certain she believed in his feelings for her. No words formed. His apprehension was fueled by how easily she could excite him, how unsuspectingly happy she seemed.

She moved closer and kissed him. Her lips were sticky and delicious, the taste of chocolate and marshmallow adding to the erotic warmth and feel of her mouth.

Within seconds they were lying on the blanket, wrapped in each other's arms, their kisses growing heated and demanding.

"Justin," she said, easing away and bracketing his face, "why don't we go to my room and fill the whirlpool?"

Her kisses had him aroused, but those words

shot pure lust through his veins. Thoughts of being naked with her in a tub of slick warm water tied him in knots. Last night he'd been free to take what she offered and enjoy it to the fullest. Last night he'd been blissfully unaware of her situation and his part in it.

Tonight he had no excuse. If he made love with her the way he wanted to, he would be underhanded and dishonest.

"There's nothing I'd like more," he said with sincerity.

She smiled, pressed a hard kiss to his lips and pushed to her knees.

But he had to tell her.

She looked at him curiously.

Justin sat up. He would rather take a beating than say what he had to say. He would endure anything if it would change the facts. He hadn't called Terrence back, hadn't figured out how this would play out. And today he'd even considered resigning from his job.

"Let's go in," he said finally.

He scooped sand on the fire, made sure it was extinguished and they gathered their belongings. Justin stored the supplies in the back of his Lexus and Meredith handed him bags and blankets.

Taking her hand, he glanced toward the front desk as they passed, but no one paid them any attention as they made their way to her room and kicked off their shoes and socks inside the door.

Meredith ran warm water, added bubbles and turned on the jets. She produced candles for Justin to light and set around the edge of the whirlpool, then she turned off the lights.

Heat pooled in Justin's belly at the seductive setting. *Tell her,* intoned a voice inside his head. He would. As soon as the time seemed right.

She tugged her sweatshirt off over her head with her back to him. Watching her in the semidarkness, he removed his shirt.

She removed her bra next and tossed it on the floor. Her jeans and panties came next, baring her slim waist and curvy buttocks.

Immediately aroused, he fumbled with his jeans and had them and his boxers off in record time.

She glanced timidly over her shoulder, then stepped into the tub and lowered herself into the mountain of suds. He barely caught a glimpse of her in the mirror as she shielded her breasts.

Justin climbed in less delicately and the bubbles rose even higher.

"Your watch," she reminded him.

He unfastened the clasp and placed the timepiece on the edge of the tub.

Meredith took a thick white washcloth from a stack in the corner, wet it and squeezed gel onto it.

Glancing at the tile ledge, he noted she'd remembered to bring one of the condoms. His head buzzed with anticipation. She sat within the V of his legs with her knees raised so she could get close and proceeded to soap his neck, shoulders and chest. He immediately recognized the scent. "Coffee?"

She chuckled. "Would you believe cappuccino? Chaney gave it to me. There's body lotion, too."

"I like that girl without even meeting her," he said. He leaned forward to kiss her.

The kiss was warm and lazy, and teased his senses.

She ended it to sit back, brought one foot in contact with his erection and teased him mercilessly. Between the warm water and her caress, beads of perspiration formed on his face.

She obviously noticed, because she raised the washcloth and squeezed it out so that water ran over his skin. Moving to straddle him, she kissed his wet lips.

Her shoulders and arms were slim and white in the candlelight, her shiny hair held in a haphazard knot that allowed becoming tendrils to escape.

His good intentions were lost in the haze of arousal she created. Guilt nagged at the back of his conscience, but didn't dim his ardor. He would tell her. But he would call Terrence first and quit Children's Connection. Then she wouldn't doubt his integrity. Then he'd be free to continue this relationship without reserve.

"Can we manage it right here?" she asked on a ragged breath.

"Anywhere. Any way."

She smiled that seductively provocative smile he loved and he was lost. Silky wet skin glistened, water splashed, bodies slid and strained and the only coherent words spoken were those of praise and pleasure.

Some time later he reclined in the tub and she leaned back against him. The jets propelled soothing hot water around their sated bodies, relaxing their muscles.

She turned her face over her shoulder and he leaned to kiss her soft lips. She raised a wet hand and placed it against his jaw. He turned his lips into it.

Meredith leisurely stretched out and placed a foot on the edge of the tub.

She sat up abruptly. "Oh, no!"

"What's wrong?"

"Your watch! I knocked it into the water!"

"It'll be okay."

She fished at the bottom of the tub until she found it and brought the gold piece up. Grabbing a dry washcloth from the stack, she dried it.

"Don't worry about it," he told her.

"Justin, I've noticed your watch, and I know it's expensive."

"Well, then, it's probably waterproof."

"Does it say?" She studied the face closely, turned

it over and angled it toward the candlelight. "Is this inscription from your wife?"

A shot of awareness needled its way into his mind and he cringed in silent horror. *No!* It was too late.

"'With appreciation, Children's Connection,'" she read aloud. Confusion registered on her pretty face. Then dawning realization. She raised those penetrating hazel eyes to his. "Children's Connection?"

Fourteen

"Everything I told you last night was the truth," he blurted. "It's still true."

"What?"

With concentrated effort, he quickly assembled his thoughts. He'd already screwed up and planted doubt with those words.

Her guarded gaze bored into his. "How are you associated with Children's Connection?"

"Hell," he said, rubbing a hand down his jaw, "you're never going to believe me."

"Try me."

"I was going to tell you that I work for Children's Connection. I'm their corporate attorney. But you have to believe that I didn't know until this morning that you were—"

"You're the lawyer for the *clinic?*" she asked incredulously.

He sat forward and nodded.

Her frown revealed shock, then more questions. "You know about…about Anna?"

"I didn't put it together until I spoke with Terrence Logan this morning."

"So you're here on the tab of the clinic, too?"

"Well," he said, hastily backpedaling, "they provide suites for executives…and their lawyer."

"Did they know you were here?"

"Yes."

She stared at him in disbelief.

"But I didn't know you were here until this morning. Terrence just dumped it on me. The board has some other pressing matters to deal with and they need closure on this situation."

"This 'situation' is my *life!*" she said, anger having risen in her voice. She got to her feet, splashing water and climbing out of the tub to grab a towel and wrap it around her body. "You know the Logans, do you?"

"Terrence and I have been friends and associates for several years."

"How convenient."

"I know it seems that way—"

"And how convenient that you and I just happened

to be vacationing in the same place at the same time." Her sarcasm plainly revealed hurt, and it was killing him to have to inflict it.

"I know how it looks."

"The board needs some closure to this embarrassing little 'situation,' do they? How selfish of me to keep them waiting. So they sent their top gun! Along with his entire family, so that I'd be completely unsuspecting that they'd decided to tighten the screws to persuade me I didn't want to sue or hold anyone to blame for their mistake."

Her voice shook with emotion and unshed tears. Regret and frustration gnawed through his composure.

"Their 'mistake' is my child," she said on a sob, then caught herself and continued. "My precious little baby girl."

"I know, Meredith—"

"You can go back and set their minds at ease. My mother is the one who wanted to sue, not me. She's the one who's been hounding them to admit their responsibility and who pressured me to give up Anna for adoption so as not to cause her humiliation. Well, I refused to do as she demanded and I don't want to sue, either. All I want is to be certain that the baby I carried for nine months is really my child."

Lord, she had *that* question hanging over her, as well? He had no idea. The full extent of her situation was like a sudden punch to his gut.

She wrapped her arms around herself. "Oh, she's my child. I carried her in my body and I gave birth to her and I *love* her…but I don't know for certain that she was conceived with my own eggs. If they screwed up the sperm, they could have messed up my eggs, as well."

All her pain and uncertainty was evident in those words. "You certainly have every right to know that," he said, feeling ineffective and powerless and hating it.

"Damn right I do. And I have a right to my privacy. And I have a right to do as I damn well please without being coerced and—and *seduced* into compliance!"

He reacted with defensive anger, but he concealed it. "I did not seduce you. What we did was mutual. And I didn't know who you were at the time. I swear to you. I was going to tell you as soon as I resigned from Children's Connection."

She looked at him as though she was considering his words, as though she wanted to believe them— believe in him. But then her expression hardened once again. "Right. There are so many other single white mothers with half-black babies at this hotel."

She turned to leave the room.

Justin, who'd been too stunned to move until that moment, lunged out of the tub and stopped her. Water streamed down his body and soaked the tiled floor. "I didn't know they'd invited you here."

She shrugged his wet hand from her arm and wouldn't look at him. "Don't touch me."

That command had the power to slice him in half.

"And don't expect me to believe that you weren't here to soften me up. If you'd been honest with me, I'd have told you I had no intention of a lawsuit. Suing the clinic would be acknowledging that Anna is a mistake. And she's not. Tell them that."

"Of course she's not."

"And tell them that all I want now is reassurance that this won't happen to someone else. I feel it's my responsibility to protect another woman."

She'd already been through so much, he knew, and she deserved better. "There will be a settlement, Meredith. The clinic is prepared to offer you a substantial amount."

"I think the clinic's given me quite enough already. So you—" she pointed a finger at his bare chest "—get out and stay the hell away from me."

In her mind, he was the enemy now. By some cosmic joke he'd gone from lover to traitor in the span of minutes. "Meredith!" he shouted to her retreating back.

She didn't stop. She ran into the bedroom and slammed the door, locking it. Like a fanned flame, anger rose up and seared his thoughts. This was not his fault, damn it!

He grabbed a towel and hastily dried off, then yanked on his pants and stormed to the bedroom door. "Meredith, talk to me."

Silence.

"I was going to tell you, I swear. Let me explain."

The door opened and she emerged dressed, her hair brushed into order. "I'm going to get Anna. If you're not gone when I get back, I'll call and have you removed."

Her threat was too strong to ignore. "I'll call you in the morning," he said to her retreating back.

He put on his shoes, grabbed the rest of his clothes and stormed out to the beach, where the waves continued their eternal journey, lapping against the shore.

"I thought you'd be later," Mauli said when she opened the door to Meredith's knock.

"No," Meredith replied, struggling to keep her composure. "I'll go get her."

She found Anna sleeping on Mauli's bed and carried her out of the room. She deliberately avoided looking at the room where the boys were sleeping, and when she gave Mauli an impulsive hug, she knew the girl could feel her trembling.

Mauli looked at her curiously. "Are you okay?"

Meredith shook her head. "I can't explain. Thanks for everything, Mauli. I don't know when I'll see you again."

"Why? What's wrong?"

"You'll have to ask Justin to explain. Just remember that your friendship has meant a lot to me." She turned and escaped out the door and down the hall, praying she wouldn't run into Justin, that the elevator would come and he wouldn't be on it.

He wasn't, and she entered, holding her baby close and crying freely now. He'd wanted her to believe that he hadn't known who she was—and she'd wanted to. Her heart begged her to listen to his pleas and accept his innocence.

But past experience and a healthy dose of self-protectiveness overruled and steered her emotions. *Fool me once, shame on you; fool me twice, shame on me.*

Her door was locked, the room unoccupied, and she breathed a sigh of relief. She placed the still-sleeping Anna in her crib and wiped up the sopping wet mess in the bathroom. Stripping off her clothing, she couldn't hold back the sobs. Her thoughts wouldn't even come together to make sense or reason. She'd been tricked. And she'd been so needy that she'd lapped up the attention and the line of bull. How appallingly desperate of her.

How inexcusable and unforgivable of him to lead her on and play with her heart. How cold and calculating of him, and how stupid of her to be so susceptible.

She was a world-class chump.

And how pathetic that she wanted to believe his denial.

She never wanted to see him again.

Throwing wet towels into a pile, she shook with anger—and cried for what she'd thought had been.

Justin Weber worked for Children's Connection! But how could she have known?

As the bubbles in the tub dissipated, she discovered the watch, which had fallen back into the water unnoticed. She picked it up and stared at it with blurry vision.

Never in a million years would she have had reason to suspect he was anyone other than who he appeared. He was so good...so believable....

She'd shared more than her body with him; she'd shared her inhibitions, her hopes and her fears...and he'd seemed so sincere. All the more fuel to add to this gut-wrenchingly deep hurt and betrayal. How could her chest ache this badly when it felt so empty?

When she blew out the candles and went to turn down the bed, there were no more tears left to be cried. Her throat hurt and her head pounded, and she felt as though she'd run miles carrying a heavy burden. Pausing only to check on Anna, she collapsed on the bed and fell into exhausted slumber.

I think the clinic's given me quite enough already. So you stay the hell away from me. Meredith's words and the look on her face had kept him awake all night. She didn't believe him and why should she? If he'd have read her file himself, rather than passing it along to his assistant—if he'd have been more *involved,* he would have realized who she was and could have prevented what had happened. There wasn't enough regret in the world to make up for that.

He'd slept with the Malone woman. Even Terrence wouldn't believe he had no ulterior motive.

No, it had been an avalanche of errors all the way around. A monumental miscommunication he should have prevented. Or had the board intended something similar? Not Terrence; his friend wasn't underhanded or manipulative. So how could this have happened?

After shaving and showering early, he dressed and ventured out into the sitting room. He'd just ordered coffee when Mauli joined him. "What happened between you and Meredith?" she asked without hesitation.

Justin backed up to the desk and rested his hip. "I don't know if you'll believe me."

"Try me."

He couldn't tell her the details of Meredith's case, so he was inhibited in what he could reveal. Meredith's connection to the clinic was private, so he merely explained that he hadn't realized Meredith was party to a legal suit in one of his cases. He'd belatedly found out, but she'd believed he'd taken advantage of her.

"Did you take advantage of her?" Mauli asked, her gaze narrowed.

"No," he replied. "I had no idea. And when I did find out, I planned to resign and then tell her. She found out first."

She absorbed his reply. "I guess she has reasons for her lack of trust, huh?"

Justin nodded. "I guess she does."

"And I'm sure she's pretty hurt and thinks she has good cause for her feelings."

He nodded again. "She wants me to leave her alone."

"Maybe she really wants you to talk to her, but she's too hurt and mad right now."

"I don't have much to lose, do I?" He took a couple of bills from his pocket. "Tip room service, will you?"

He headed toward the elevator and down to Meredith's room. As soon as he raised his hand to the door, his heart thudded. He knocked. And waited.

Knocked again. No response.

Back in his room, he dialed hers, but the call didn't go through. Instead, a recording told him the room was unoccupied.

Dreading what he would learn, Justin called the desk. "I'm trying to reach Miss Malone in room seven."

"Miss Malone checked out this morning," the desk clerk responded. "She left an envelope for you at the desk. I'll send someone right up with it."

A few minutes later, he tipped the staff member, ripped open the bulky envelope and stared at his watch.

The fog under the watch face matched the one in his mind. He deliberately cleared his thoughts. "Mauli, what's her cell phone number?"

Mauli handed him a slip of paper and he punched in the numbers. He got Meredith's voice mail and hung up without leaving a message.

Lamond appeared in the doorway in his Spider-Man pajamas. "What are we gonna do today, Dad?"

Fifteen

What a difference a day made. All of Justin's loyalties lay on the line now. Terrence was his friend and the clinic his livelihood. Meredith was the woman to whom he'd made spoken and unspoken promises. His children and his future were caught somewhere in between.

He was angry with the board of directors for their thoughtless part in this. No, they hadn't anticipated he'd become involved with the woman, but they'd underhandedly maneuvered a meeting.

He was disgusted with himself for not taking a more active and comprehensive role in Meredith Malone's case. All of this could have been prevented if he'd recognized her name when he'd met her. It would even have had a better outcome if he hadn't been too cowardly to tell her as soon as he'd learned the truth.

He was hurt that she hadn't listened to him or given him the benefit of the doubt about his part in being at the same place at the same time. But then she didn't have much cause to trust. Add the facts that her fiancé had dumped on her and her own mother didn't support her, he guessed the sum was a general lack of trust in people.

She didn't know him well enough to know his brand of integrity, and he hadn't had much of a chance to earn her confidence. What they'd shared had been too new and tentative to handle that devastating news with any real conviction.

What Justin feared now was that Meredith would never give him a chance to prove himself or to work things out. He would have to deal with that, as well as his part in it.

Thinking about losing her so quickly made him angry. Maybe it was for the best in the long run. Anyone who could so completely misunderstand his motives was probably not a person he needed in his life.

He tried to tell that to his heart, too, but so far it wasn't listening.

After answering perceptively curious questions, he was left to deal with his boys' disappointment over Meredith's leave-taking. The week passed a bit more slowly and uneventfully than the first, and when it was time to head home, they were all ready. He arrived back in Portland on Friday, so he'd have the weekend to organize himself and the family before getting back into the work and school routine.

Every day he had called her cell phone, listened to her voice-mail message and hung up. Finally Monday, on his way to work, he left a message: "Meredith, it's Justin. I understand your feelings and your lack of trust, I do. I'd appreciate it if you'd talk to me. We could meet somewhere for coffee. We could meet anywhere. Or you could just answer the phone or return my call." And, covering all the bases, he left numbers for his office, his home and his cell.

He'd just left the message, so when his phone rang, his heart skipped a nervous beat.

But it was his own office number on the caller ID. "Good morning, Alicia."

"Good morning, Mr. Weber. How was your vacation?" The voice of his fiftyish secretary was cheerful and familiar.

"It was good," he replied. "The boys were almost worn out."

She laughed good-naturedly. "Then you must have done something right."

"What's up? I didn't think I had anything scheduled this morning."

"You don't. I kept the calendar free so you could catch up. But Morgan Davis just called and asked to see you."

She referred to director of the Children's Connection. "Did he say what about?"

"Only that it was important that he speak with you."

Justin glanced at his bare wrist before he remembered his watch needed repair and still lay on his dresser. He glanced at the clock on the dash. "I'm on my way in. Tell him I'll be there in about ten minutes."

"Will do. Do you want lunch brought in today or do you have plans?"

"Keep me open."

"Done. See you when you get here."

Justin ended the call and drove toward the clinic. Inside the office area, which was decorated in muted pastels and supplied with comfortable chairs, the receptionist greeted him. "Mr. Davis is expecting you," she said and got up to lead him down a hallway to a set of double doors. She rapped on the wood, opened the door and preceded him in. "Mr. Weber is here, sir."

"Morning, Justin," Morgan Davis said, standing to shake his hand.

The woman handed Justin a cup of black coffee and discreetly disappeared.

"How was your vacation?" Morgan asked politely.

"It was the best of times, it was the worst of

times," he replied, taking a seat and sipping the steaming coffee.

"You're rested?"

"Physically."

"I see." Morgan came around to sit in the chair beside him. "I understand Terrence filled you in on the FBI investigation."

"He did. Any new developments?"

"No, but information is trickling in. Apparently several kidnappers were captured in a sting in Russia. However, the police in Moscow aren't sharing much information or any names, so the Feds are starting from scratch."

"And the Sanders baby is still missing?"

"I'm afraid so."

"What's his name?"

Morgan cast Justin a look of surprise.

"The missing baby is a boy, right? What's his name?"

"Timothy," Morgan replied.

"Sanders is the name of the birth mother, correct?"

Morgan nodded. "Lisa Sanders. A troubled girl who was living with the adoptive parents."

"And the adoptive parents' names are?"

"Brian and Carrie Summers."

"The baby was taken from the hospital shortly after his birth?"

"Stolen from the nursery."

Justin absorbed the information, deliberately re-membering the people involved as individuals. "There was an incident here last fall. An attempt to snatch a baby who was being given up for adoption."

Morgan nodded. "Ivy Crosby was bringing a baby from the hospital to our nursery. She was fighting off the offenders when I heard the struggle and ran out. An odd-looking pair—man and woman—got away."

"Isn't Ivy a Crosby Systems executive? What was she doing with a baby?"

"She volunteers with the crack babies—has a real gift. That particular child was being placed for adoption."

"The police were unable to help?"

"The couple disappeared with no trace."

"But now it looks as though these cases are related."

"I'm afraid so," Morgan replied. He ran a hand over his hair before continuing. "And just when I think things are as bad as they can get, something else proves me wrong."

"Has something happened to another baby?"

"No, this is more on the Malone situation."

"Meredith Malone," Justin clarified, apprehensive at the mention of her name. "What's wrong?"

"Wayne Thorpe came to me with a confession."

What could the wealthy retiree who served on the board of directors have to confess that would make Meredith's situation worse? Justin waited impatiently.

"It seems he's been...keeping company with Sheila Crosby."

"Sleeping with her?" Justin asked.

Morgan nodded.

Ex-wife of Jack Crosby, the founder of Crosby Systems, Sheila had the reputation of being the neglectful mother who hadn't been paying attention to her own son or to the Logans' boy Robbie the day he'd been kidnapped. Talk was she'd always been selfish and narcissistic, and had turned the whole kidnapping situation around to make it look as though she was the victim. She had several children who'd grown up successfully despite her parenting, and now Sheila spent her time squandering her settlement from Jack in Portland and in Palm Springs, where she lived part-time.

"How is she involved in this?"

"You know the Logans and the Crosbys have been rivals for years."

Justin nodded.

"And that Sheila was supposed to be watching the Logans' boy the day he was taken."

"Yes."

"She hates the Logans for her misconstrued opinion of how bad they made her look. She would do anything to disgrace or lay them low and she'd do it gleefully."

"What's the connection?"

"Wayne came to me in a fit of regret. It seems he

tends to drink and when he drinks, he says more than he should."

Justin stood and walked to the window. He stared out at the deceivingly bright day. Dread grasped him by the short hairs. "Thorpe let the sperm mix-up slip and now Sheila Crosby knows," he guessed.

"Unfortunately," Morgan confirmed.

Justin exhaled on a curse. "What has she done?"

"Nothing yet that I know of. That was last night and Wayne called me at first light this morning. Justin, we can't let the information get out this way."

His thoughts of resigning were out of the question with this at stake. All business now, Justin turned back to face Morgan. "We have to hit her where she hurts. What leverage do we have? She doesn't care about her kids…. What do we know about her?"

Morgan pressed his intercom button. "We'll go to the source. Office gossip. Cora, what do you know about Sheila Crosby?"

The receptionist took only seconds to reply. "She's a shopoholic and she's had everything on her body tucked or lifted or enhanced. She manages to attract rich men, but none of her relationships last. She picks guys who have money and social status and she loves the country club. Her grown children mostly work for Crosby Systems, that is Ivy, Katie and Trent. Danny is some kind of a rich recluse and nobody knows much about him." She finally paused for a breath. "That what you wanted to know, Mr. Davis?"

Morgan couldn't help a smile. "That's good, thanks." He clicked off the intercom and said to Justin, "Trent took Jack's place as CEO of Crosby Systems."

"Jack wouldn't give a damn if the Logans or the clinic got bad publicity." The nearly thirty-year feud between the Crosbys and the Logans was legendary.

"But Trent is decent and responsible. He might be an ally."

Morgan stood and filled his coffee mug. "What leverage would he hold over his mother?"

Justin felt a glimmer of satisfaction. "What does she care most about?"

"Money. Social status. The country club."

"And who is membership chair of the country club?"

Morgan set down the coffee pot and turned. "Trent Crosby."

Bingo.

Leaving Anna at the hospital's day care was an emotional experience, but the staff, and especially the caregiver assigned to Anna, were encouraging and helpful. Darla Adams was a sweet-faced young woman with a smile that lit her dimpled features. She immediately snuggled Anna close and spoke to her. "We're going to have a great time together, aren't we? I have a crib all ready for you and a special teddy bear with your name on his shirt. Look."

She showed Anna the bright blue stuffed animal sporting a yellow T-shirt with Anna's name in red embroidery.

A quick glance around the facility showed a similar bear in each child's crib. The babies already present seemed content in their Excersaucers and in the mesh playpens. The rooms were bright and clean, and the staff cheerful.

"Call anytime you like," Darla said.

Anna only stared in wide-eyed wonder as Meredith kissed her goodbye and swallowed back tears.

Her first day back was a flurry of welcomes, cards and flowers, and the usual adjustments. In between patients and paperwork, she visited the day care. On her lunch hour, she hurried down to nurse her, and by the time her shift was over, she was exhausted.

Turning into her driveway, she spotted the familiar dark cherry Lexus SUV at the curb in front of her house.

Sixteen

Anxiety rose inside as she pulled into her garage and shut off the engine. Taking Anna and her bag from the car, she stepped outside.

Justin had placed two enormous boxes on her lawn, and a spade lay beside them. Seeing him made it painfully clear how lonely she'd been since leaving Cannon Beach. "What are you doing?"

"Hello, Anna," he said to the baby.

The infant's responsive smile at the sound of his voice gave Meredith an added twinge in the area of her heart.

"Nice to see you, too," he said to Meredith.

"I told you I didn't want to see you."

He turned and gestured. "Your wind art has been at my place for a few days. I thought I'd better come over and set it up for you. We did ours yesterday."

"That wasn't necessary."

"It was in my garage."

She had completely forgotten. "You can just leave it here, then."

"Tell me where you want it. It only takes a few minutes to dig a couple of holes and set the anchors. I'll be careful of your lawn."

She glanced around. "Up there at the front of the house."

"Good choice. That way you can watch it from your picture window."

She turned back to enter the house through the garage and closed the overhead door behind her. Inside, she made Anna comfortable in her seat on the kitchen floor and set about fixing herself some supper.

While she waited for the microwave, she tiptoed into her living room and covertly watched Justin from behind the curtains. At least he hadn't brought the boys; that would have been dirty play on his part. As it was, she had enough trouble seeing only him and not giving in to missing him. How painfully ironic that she was self-protectively shutting out the very people who had been the most accepting of her and Anna.

Back in the kitchen, she ate her microwave dinner and a pear with a glass of milk, then wiped the counter and picked up the baby.

Meredith had just taken Anna to her room and changed her diaper when the doorbell rang.

Meredith snapped up her daughter's clothing and placed her in her crib before she walked through the house to the door.

Justin stepped back from the opening and gestured. "All done."

She peered out at the metal sculpture she had chosen, its graceful arms slowly turning in the breeze. Would she always feel this bitter sense of loss when she looked at it? "Thanks."

"No problem."

He studied her and his gaze made her uncomfortable. "May I talk to you for a few minutes?"

"I don't think so. Nothing you can say will change what happened and the way it happened." As much as she regretted that, it was the truth.

"I'd like a chance to change what you believe about me."

"And you're good at counterarguments, I'll give you that. Maybe I don't want my mind changed."

"I just know we had something good."

She couldn't argue there'd been something good between them. Still...it didn't change the facts. She steeled herself and raised her chin. "It's easy for you to say you didn't know who I was. It's not so easy for me to believe it. It's also easy to say you were going to tell me, but the fact remains, you didn't. So what am I supposed to think, Justin?"

"I know how bad it looks, Meredith."

"Yes, it does."

"I don't know how to convince you that I was unaware you were…" He stopped and a muscle in his jaw worked.

"I was what?"

"That you were the Malone woman. You never told me your last name."

She thought back and tried to remember if that was true, but she had no recollection.

"I learned something about myself that I didn't like very much," he admitted.

She wasn't going to ask, but he went on anyway.

"I was caught up in my caseload and court schedules and all the surrounding details, and I wasn't seeing the people involved. I'm ashamed of that."

She tried to comprehend.

"Maybe it's unprofessional to be involved in cases on a personal level. Maybe there's a happy medium there somewhere, but I was so far below the medium that I barely knew people's names. That was my fault. If I'd been involved on more than a superficial level, this wouldn't have happened. So, I'm sorry. I wanted to say that."

No matter how contrite Justin was, nothing could

take away the overwhelming sense of betrayal and the hurt she'd experienced. Besides, even if she wanted to believe him, how could she? It was easier to not have to place her trust in anyone.

If she'd been more vigilant about looking out for herself, she would have remembered that and not foolishly fallen into the situation.

A red car swept into her driveway, drawing her attention. Chaney got out and walked toward the small porch. She stepped up beside Justin and looked from him to Meredith with a question in her expression. "Hi, I'm Chaney."

"Justin Weber," he said, moving aside to greet her.

"I've never met a nine-and-a-half in the flesh before." She stuck out her hand and he shook it.

One of Justin's eyebrows rose quizzically.

Meredith ignored her friend's comment and Justin's look. "He was just leaving," she pointed out.

"Don't go on my account," Chaney said, eyeing him up and down.

"I brought over Meredith's wind sculpture."

Chaney glanced toward the metal artwork in the yard. "You're handy, too. Awesome."

"Come on in," Meredith said and made room for her friend to pass. She turned back to Justin for a brief dismissal. "Thank you. Goodbye."

"I'll call you," he said.

"I probably won't answer."

"I've already figured that out. But I'm hoping."

She met his gaze for what seemed a lengthy time and finally stepped in and closed the door.

Chaney ran to the window and watched him walk away and place the spade in his car. "Oh. My. God."

Meredith nodded.

"He looks so sincere. And he came all the way over here to set up that gizmo for you. He just came to see you, you know, he could have had it sent or left it on your porch."

"I know."

"What did he say?"

"That he was sorry and he didn't know how to convince me he didn't know who I was when we met."

"What did you say?"

"There wasn't much to say. I just can't believe him. Even if he did just find out that morning, he still didn't tell me."

"I can see where that would be a tough thing to stick into a conversation."

"I got *naked* with him. I let him see my scars. I *trusted* him."

"That's what hurt the most, wasn't it? You felt vulnerable, but you wanted him. You moved your own safety parameters aside to let him get close."

That was what still hurt. "It's my own fault, when you say it like that."

"Take a little responsibility, Mer."

"Okay."

"He's gone." Chaney moved away from the window. "Takes your breath away just looking at the man, doesn't it?"

Meredith nodded.

"Where's my girl?"

"In her bed."

"Awake? How did day care go?"

Meredith followed her to Anna's room, relating their first time at day care and her return to work.

Chaney stayed for a while, giving Anna a bath and then doing a load of laundry while Meredith fed the baby and put her to bed. As Chaney prepared to leave, she gave her friend a hug. "I want you to remember something."

Meredith returned her hug and drew away. "What?"

"Remember that Justin Weber is not Sean."

"I know that."

"On an intellectual level you know that, but are you emotionally aware? Sean was a first-class rat. He left you high and dry because he couldn't deal with your illness and recovery. He didn't want to stand by or help make critical decisions or be supportive. He's a weasel. This thing with Denzel isn't remotely similar."

Meredith rolled her eyes.

"Seriously," Chaney went on. "Does he seem the type to desert a person when the chips are down?"

"I don't know enough about him to make that assessment," Meredith replied. "I do know he's an eloquent speaker and a top-notch attorney. Convincing people to see things his way is his job."

Chaney squeezed Meredith's hands and released them. "What if I learned something life changing? What if I was trying to figure out how to tell you without breaking your heart, but you found out some other way first? Would you think I was untrustworthy, too?"

"That's not a fair comparison. I've known you a long time, and I already know you have my best interests at heart. I don't know that about Justin."

"Isn't this the same guy you said was so great with his kids?" Chaney asked.

"Yes."

"Then do you really think he's a totally different person with you?"

Meredith shrugged. "I don't know. People aren't always what they seem."

"Bull. A week ago, you couldn't say enough nice things about the man." Chaney opened the front door and turned back with a grin. "And I know sex isn't everything, but if that man had the hots for me, I'd make a lot of exceptions to keep him in *my* bed."

Meredith returned the smile, then called to her friend's retreating back, "But, then, you're confident and well-adjusted and I'm a skeptical neurotic. Good night."

* * *

The following week she received notice in the mail from the laboratory who'd done the DNA tests on her and Anna as soon as they'd returned from Cannon Beach. The results read probability 98.2%.

Meredith wept with relief. She'd known all along in her heart that Anna was her child, but she'd needed this concrete evidence to set her mind at ease. Whoever Anna's father was didn't matter. It hadn't mattered when she'd anticipated he was white, so it didn't matter now that she knew he wasn't.

With the big uncertainty behind her and her decisions made, she had one chore left—to settle things with her mother. She'd spoken briefly with her father, promising to call him for a visit, so she made the call now.

"Dad?"

"Hi, honey. How're you doing?"

"Much better now that I have proof that Anna is really my child."

"The DNA test?"

"Yes, it was positive beyond a doubt."

"That's wonderful." Meredith could practically hear her father's smile.

"Yes, it is," she agreed. "How's Veronica?"

Her dad's voice sobered. "She's her usual self. Busy. Gone."

"I thought I'd fix dinner tomorrow night and you could come over and see us. Think she'll come?"

"I'll ask her," he said. "She's still mad that you stopped taking her calls."

"I was on vacation." Knowing her excuse was lame, she thought again. "You know, it's not fair of me to ask you to be the go-between, so ask her to call me when she gets home, okay?"

"Will do. Bye, honey."

It was later that evening when the phone rang and Meredith saw her folks' name on the caller ID. "Hello?"

"You've unblocked our number, I see." Veronica's tone was aloof.

"I needed time to think."

"With all that thinking, have you come to your senses?"

Meredith took a deep breath to build her resolve. "I'd like to talk to you and Dad. Will you come for dinner tomorrow evening?"

"What is it you want to say?"

"I'd rather talk in person. Can you come at six-thirty?"

"Unless you're planning to tell us that you're bringing suit against that negligent clinic," Veronica said, "I don't know that we have anything to discuss."

Under her breath, Meredith counted to ten. "I'm making one last attempt to salvage a relationship here. If you don't want it, say so."

Her mother was silent for a moment. "Six-thirty." Then she hung up.

* * *

The following day at lunch, pediatric OR nurse Rebecca Holley joined Meredith in the cafeteria. They had worked together with patients many times and maintained a professional friendship.

"I'm treating a patient you'll remember." Meredith went on to tell Rebecca that one of her young patients was doing well in his therapy and recovery.

"That's fantastic news. He has a great outlook and terrific parents, too."

"It's always rewarding to see children in recovery do so well. Sometimes the results are not as promising."

Rebecca nodded knowingly. "I haven't talked with you about your camp for a while. How are the plans going?"

"Plans have been on hold, I'm afraid. But it's time to get back at it."

"I'd like to help any way I can."

Her offer warmed Meredith's heart. "I'd appreciate your help."

"What's the biggest need right now?"

"Money," she replied easily.

"Okay. Make me your fund-raising chairperson."

"Really?"

Rebecca nodded and took a pad and pen from the pocket of her teddy-bear-print smock. "Really. Let's make a list of contacts and prepare a letter. We'll share the follow-up."

By the time Meredith went back upstairs to work, ideas had come to life and her hopes had been renewed. She felt more focused than she had in weeks. It was time to move on with her life.

When she got home she prepared dinner, set the table and had just finished feeding Anna when her parents arrived.

Her father immediately picked up Anna from the playpen and held her on his lap. Her mother refused to look at the baby.

When Veronica asked about her vacation, Meredith didn't have much she wanted to share. The rest of their conversation was equally stilted.

Eventually, Meredith ushered them into her dining room, where she propped Anna in her seat on the unused end of the table.

Her father dug into his dinner, but her mother merely picked at the vegetables. Finally she laid down her fork. "When are you going to get to the point and say whatever it is we've come to hear?"

Meredith took a sip of water and dabbed her lips. "I've made all my decisions and nothing is going to change my mind."

Veronica pursed her lips. "You always were a stubborn girl."

She let that pass and continued. "I am not going to sue Children's Connection. I do not want any publicity or any compensation. I'm prepared to simply ask them to refund any and all medical costs involved with the in vitro and the DNA testing."

"So you'll allow everyone to believe she's your child?"

"She *is* my child."

"But, Meredith." Veronica's eyes showed her distress. "People will believe that you…had relations with a black man." She said the last two words in a whisper as though it was too shameful to say aloud.

"That's just fine with me," Meredith replied.

Veronica's eyebrows shot to her hairline.

"A few of my co-workers and close friends were aware that I was going through the in vitro process," Meredith explained. "And I don't particularly care what strangers think. My biggest concern was whether or not I'd be able to provide Anna with the support and confidence she needed to grow up as a child of mixed race.

"But now I know that I can do it and that there are people who will help me. She's going to get a lot of stares and hear many questions and face prejudice in her life. I can't prevent that, and you don't know how it hurts me to think of it.

"But I can prepare her. And I can provide an environment of friends and loved ones to see her through the adjustments."

With both elbows on the table, Meredith laced her fingers and looked directly into her mother's eyes. "There are a few ways I can protect her. No matter what she is faced with from the world, she will never hear those things or be made to feel unwanted or alienated by me or my family or my friends."

At those words, Veronica's demeanor changed. A look of hurt stole over her features.

Meredith didn't let it stop her. "If you can't accept Anna, then you won't be a part of our lives. I won't allow your bigotry to hurt her. I want her to have grandparents. But I *will* protect her."

Meredith's father had lain down his fork. He cleared his throat. "I'll help any way I can. I can come over here to help with her if I need to." He glanced at his wife, then back to his daughter. "She's my granddaughter and I love her. Don't keep her from me because of your mother."

Grateful for his steadfast devotion, she gave him a warm smile. "I won't, Dad. Thank you."

Veronica sat in stunned silence for another minute, confusion plain on her face. Meredith knew what she was thinking. Her only daughter had just set the rules for their continued relationship, while her husband had made his position clear. Finally Veronica looked up. "No one has ever called me a bigot before. I don't believe I like it."

Meredith shrugged.

"I—I just don't know what I'll say to my friends, the women at bridge club and our...well, *anyone*."

"What have you said so far?"

"Nothing," Veronica admitted.

"Well, you can continue to say nothing. It's no one's business, anyway. If you feel like explaining, tell them your daughter chose to have this baby and that you chose to support her." Meredith couldn't help the next word. "Please."

Her mother met her eyes and tried again. "What about the emotional distress? Surely that's worth a suit."

"*You're* the one causing me emotional distress," she said plainly. "I'm not embarrassed by Anna or ashamed of her. And it breaks my heart to think that you are." Impulsively, Meredith rose to pick up the baby from her seat. Delighted, Anna smiled and waved a fist.

Without a word of warning, Meredith walked around the table and placed the baby in her mother's arms. Veronica had never even held her, and Meredith was tired of feeling hurt and angry.

Obviously caught off guard, her mother sat back to accommodate the child.

"Look at her. Look into her eyes. She's just a baby," Meredith told her. "An innocent little person who had no say in her conception or birth. She deserves love and acceptance. She needs a family."

Veronica looked down at the baby. Anna had a concentrated frown on her face as she studied the new person who held her. Suddenly, she broke into smiles and kicked her legs excitedly.

"This is it for us," Meredith said quietly. "You can choose to be Anna's grandmother...or you can choose to lose us both."

Veronica's watery gaze flickered from the gurgling baby to her daughter and back. "You've obviously made up your mind," she said finally.

Meredith's heart dipped with disappointment as she prepared to hear a hurtful remark.

But Veronica's tone was soft when she said, "You're a bright, intelligent woman, so I'm going to trust that you've made the best decision for you."

Meredith blinked. That was a huge admission for a woman so hell-bent on being right. But it wasn't quite enough. Her daughter would not be cheated and would not be made to feel lacking. "Can you love her?"

Veronica looked up at her daughter with tears in her eyes. "Yes," she whispered.

The following week, Meredith sat in the cramped office she shared with three other physical therapists and updated patient data in the computer. A knock at the open door caught her attention, and she glanced up.

Justin Weber stood in the doorway. He wore a dark three-piece suit with an ecru shirt, silk tie and shiny leather shoes. She'd never seen him in his business attire, and he seemed like a handsome stranger. She felt underdressed in her smock and slacks.

"May I have a few minutes of your time?" he asked. "It's business."

Business. The sticky little situation. "I communicated through my counselor to assure the board that I had no intention of suing. I merely asked for compensation for medical bills."

"I'm aware of that."

His appearance was all business, all the professional lawyer. She got a knot in her stomach at the memory of shared intimacies. "Do you have something for me to sign to let them off the hook? I'll sign it."

"No. This visit has nothing to do with that."

Curious, she sat back. "Oh."

He moved into the cramped office and set his leather attaché on a chair. Opening it, he withdrew a few pieces of paper, separated a small one and held it toward her. "I'm here at Leslie Logan's request. This is her personal donation to Camp I Can."

Meredith had automatically accepted the paper he offered and now realized she held a check. A check made out for an amount her brain worked to compute. Stunned, she looked up. "What is this?"

"It's for the lease on the camp. It's enough, isn't it?"

Her mind whirled, imagining what she could do with that amount of money, but at the same time her suspicions were aroused. "Of course, it's enough. But why so much? Why now?"

"The way I understand it, you've been soliciting

donations. Leslie was recently able to free up the funds to contribute."

Meredith stood and waved the check as though the ink needed drying. She couldn't help the question that rose in her mind. "And this is not intended as a juicy morsel to dangle in front of someone to ensure they don't sue the clinic?"

Justin's gaze didn't waver. "If you wanted money for yourself, you would have taken a settlement, Meredith. When Leslie and I discussed this, I warned her you'd be suspicious for only the reasons she's aware of. But she feels very strongly about helping with the camp, and I'm her attorney."

With this money she could lease the property! She could immediately start lining up medical professionals, volunteers, counselors and coaches. The money was for the kids, not for her, even though it would bring her dream into reality.

"I'll call Leslie right away to thank her," she said, deciding.

Justin closed his attaché and straightened. She wondered if he'd expected more resistance. "How is Anna?" he asked.

"She's good. She's in day care on the third floor."

"She's adjusting?"

"Quite well. How are the boys and Mauli?"

"The boys are busy with school and activities. They're both playing basketball, so Mauli and I have a schedule of practices and games we share. Mauli is the same."

Meredith absorbed thoughts of Justin's family and regret stabbed her anew. What had seemed so right and so simple had become complicated and confusing.

Justin studied her. "You can keep your friendship with Mauli and not see me, you know."

She nodded. "I'll probably call her."

"Good. The boys ask about you and Anna all the time. They want to know when they'll see you again. I don't know what to say."

She didn't know what to say, either. She had grown fond of his children and disappointing them hurt her.

He didn't make a move to leave. "If I thought it would make a difference to you, if it would convince you of my sincerity, I would resign my position at Children's Connection."

Caught off guard, she absorbed the huge sacrifice he suggested. It was beyond her comprehension why he'd consider such a drastic move. "I don't expect you to do that. What would it prove?"

"That you're important to me," he replied immediately. He looked away and then back. "I never expected to feel anything for a woman after my wife died. But I feel something for you. You haven't given me a chance to explain or apologize for what happened."

His words brought a flutter to her heart, but her

own internal confusion accompanied the sensation. "You explained plenty."

"I want to apologize."

The moment stretched out between them before she replied. "Okay."

"I'm sorry. As soon as I learned who you were I should have come straight to you instead of panicking about how you would react. I didn't do that and I regret it."

She'd been quick to jump to conclusions when she'd learned his involvement with the clinic. She hadn't given him the benefit of the doubt or listened to his apology. She did so now. Still, it was hard to trust after what she'd been through.

"I need some time," she said. "We kidded about it, but the situation at Cannon Beach was extremely romantic, to say the least. If we truly were strangers attracted to each other, and if you didn't have previous knowledge of my situation, the circumstances were still unreal."

She liked the way he listened. As though he cared and what she had to say was important. She'd never put her finger on it before, but he always listened to her this way. "Maybe my feelings were raw and I was susceptible," she continued. "You were obviously handsome and attentive, and I got caught up in the moment."

Justin's expression was suddenly stoic. "Because

if you'd been thinking clearly, you would never have become involved with *me*."

"I didn't mean it like that. I just meant maybe it was one of those things and we're better off letting it go."

"Just a fling," he said. "Over and done."

Her thoughts had come out all wrong. She hadn't meant to offend him. She wanted to believe that he had her best interests at heart and that their meeting hadn't been a scheme on his part. But could she know him well enough to be certain of his integrity?

"Justin," she said. "I'm sorry, too. I've had a lot to deal with, so many important decisions to make. I was probably not in a state of mind to begin a relationship, and I know I've handled things poorly. I'm getting my life straightened out now. I've even made progress with my mother. This—*you* are just more than I can deal with at the same time."

"You're probably right," he said. "It would take work to make our lives compatible. And I would certainly rock the boat where your mother is concerned." He picked up his attaché and took a step toward the door. "It's easier to leave things the way they are and say it was just a fling. That way nobody has to know, either."

"I'm not ashamed of anything," she denied quickly, not liking what he was insinuating.

"I didn't say you were. But it takes confidence to be in a relationship like we were contemplating. Confidence in yourself and heartfelt conviction that what you have is real and that love transcends appearances and intolerance."

She let the meaning of those words sink in, and she didn't like the way they made her feel.

Justin strode to the door and looked back. "Your trust issues go beyond men, Meredith. You don't trust yourself."

And with that, he was gone.

Seventeen

Meredith looked from the empty doorway to the check in her hand. He believed that her reluctance to throw herself at him was because he was black? How could he even think that? She'd never shown the least bit of prejudice—she was the mother of a mixed-race child! Where had he come up with such an unmerited idea?

From her previous reactions to being seen in public with him, her nagging conscience replied. Her situation with her mother. Her lack of trust in him. Her hesitancy to develop anything more permanent.

If he was so wrong, why had his words cut so

deeply and aroused her defenses? She wasn't ever afraid to work for something she wanted.

Her phone rang then, jarring her away from her problems, and she forced her mind back on work. But the rest of the day was difficult, as her thoughts kept returning to Justin and his apology, and to Leslie Logan and her generous donation.

The following day she called to schedule an appointment with Mrs. Logan. The woman suggested they get together for lunch, so Meredith met her at a restaurant near the hospital.

Leslie was a tall, slender woman of about sixty with reddish-gold hair and eyes a unique shade of brown. She greeted Meredith warmly. "I was hoping you'd bring the baby."

"I just fed her, so she's napping."

"The day care is working out?"

"Better than I imagined it would. The caregivers are fantastic. They adore Anna. Every day I get a full report of her feedings and changes and activities."

"That's so nice to hear."

They ordered and sipped their cups of tea.

"I asked to see you so that I could thank you in person for your generous donation to the camp," Meredith told her with sincere gratitude. "Your contribution is enough for the lease and much more. Camp I Can is becoming a reality, and you've helped to make it happen. So…thank you." She smiled hesitatingly. "The words seem so inadequate."

"You're quite welcome, dear. Children are one of my passions. They're our future, you know, so investing in them *is* truly investing in a better tomorrow."

"Well, a whole lot of kids are going to have a special summer experience that they'll always remember," Meredith promised her.

"Meredith, may I speak frankly?"

"Of course."

"Because of my clinic affiliations and my husband's position, I'm aware of the situation with your daughter. I have been in constant touch with your counselor. I hope you don't see that as a lack of privacy, because I assure you, I take Children's Connection seriously and I believe in patients' privacy."

"I don't have a problem with you knowing," Meredith replied easily. "It's good to know the clinic is being held accountable."

"Even though I felt a personal involvement and my heart went out, I deliberately did not approach you. There couldn't be the least shred of doubt that Children's Connection or anyone involved hadn't ever tried to influence you."

"Thank you," Meredith said.

"When our lawyer expressed his displeasure with a recent situation, I got to the bottom of it and learned that the board offered you a suite at the Lighthouse

Inn during the same weeks that he was vacationing there."

Her mention of Justin unnerved Meredith.

"My husband was very uncomfortable with the invitation and feels bad that he didn't warn Justin there could be a conflict of interest." She glanced down at her teacup, then back up to Meredith. "The board was seeking information about your intentions, but they went about it the wrong way."

Meredith's cheeks warmed. Did this woman know what had transpired? Had Justin told Terrence Logan?

"I've taken the board members to task and voiced my disappointment to my husband that he didn't stop it. Your and Justin's meeting was maneuvered and it was underhanded. I do hope no harm was caused and that you will be as gracious with this as you've been with all the other problems you've had to deal with."

"Justin truly didn't know I would be there?"

"No more than I did or I would have put a stop to it. Justin was set up, as were you, and Terrence was trapped in the middle. I know the board's intentions were good, but I don't know if the end justified the means. From what Justin said, you had no intentions of filing suit against the clinic."

"That's true."

"Well, bless you for your tolerance, dear."

"My Anna is a blessing. She's the reason for my decision."

"I hope I can meet her soon. Now, tell me more about the camp."

"The opening is months away, but I'm lining up staff and volunteers. I'm holding a meeting at the hospital next week to prepare them and to discuss positions and scenarios. If you know of anyone who'd like to donate their time, please pass along the information. There are posters and flyers up now."

"I'll certainly do that."

"As Camp I Can's benefactor, you're welcome to attend any and all meetings and, of course, the camp itself once it's open."

"Thanks for the invitation."

Meredith grinned at the woman's sincere words and humble smile. Leslie Logan was a good person with a kind heart. The adoption agency and fertility clinic wouldn't exist without her and Terrence. And Meredith was glad, because without the clinic, she wouldn't have Anna, the child of her heart.

Meredith double-checked that the coffeemakers were almost finished percolating and that the cookies and napkins were neatly arranged.

"Everything's perfect," Chaney said. "Stop obsessing."

Meredith straightened the skirt of her black suit

and glanced at the clock over the door. As she did, someone entered the meeting room. "Oh, my God, Chaney, this is it."

"Knock 'em dead, kiddo."

She hurried to greet her first volunteer, her friend Katie Crosby, whom she hadn't seen since Katie had visited her in the hospital after Anna was born. She had shared her plans for in vitro with Katie, so the young woman was one of the few people who knew how surprised Meredith had been when she'd seen her baby.

They spent a few minutes catching up, and before long the room swelled with men and women, some professionals, other lay people who just wanted to be a part of the new camp. Meredith was standing in a group with Rebecca Holley and nurse Nancy Allen when a man entering the room caught her attention.

Her heart sped up as Justin Weber greeted a few people at the rear of the room and then moved toward her.

"Good evening," he said warmly. He was dressed in a dark blue suit with a blue shirt and striped tie, looking comfortable and confident—and sexy.

She felt foolish shaking his hand, but she realized that his formal behavior was for the sake of bystanders. She made introductions. "Are you a contributor or a volunteer?" Rebecca asked Justin, snatching the question from Meredith's head.

"I'm volunteering my legal services to the camp." He turned to Meredith. "You'll need help with leases and insurance, and I'm making myself available, pro bono."

It took Meredith several seconds to find her voice. "That's incredibly generous of you."

"No more generous than anyone else here giving of their time or talents, is it?"

"No." Infinitely more unexpected, however, considering all that had happened between them, and she'd been caught off guard.

"Oh." Justin reached inside his suit jacket and withdrew a check. "One more thing. I solicited a donation for the camp on your behalf, I hope you won't mind."

Meredith looked at the check written for a substantial amount and drawn on the account of a Wayne Thorpe. "I don't know who this is."

"He's a silent benefactor who wants to help the kids."

"Well, great. Thank you."

Chaney came up to her then. "Time to start the meeting."

Meredith excused herself, the attendees took their seats and she got the informal meeting under way.

Several other donations were gifted and other volunteers stepped forward, till there were enough to staff two camps the same size. She was going to have to consider enlarging the program to enable more children to benefit.

As soon as it became clear that Justin was there

in a legal capacity, some volunteers expressed concerns about their responsibility should anything accidentally happen to a child or if there was a medical emergency they couldn't handle.

Justin capably handled the questions and took notes on a PDA, planning to draft releases for parents and guardians to sign. "I'll have contracts and release forms for you to look over next week," he told Meredith.

This was the side of Justin she'd fallen for. His openness and integrity were evident in his words and dealings.

"Next week I'm going to start taking applications," she told the assembly in closing. "The kids who will be applying have never been able to do anything remotely similar. They've been rejected from programs because of their needs. But because of your generosity," she said, looking at each face, "these kids won't be turned away. Because of the very nature of Camp I Can—and our ability to care for medical needs—children from all over will participate and feel special. Thank you from the bottom of my heart."

Rousing applause drowned out her last words.

The crowd mingled and ate cookies, and then left a few at a time, until only a handful remained.

Justin congratulated Meredith. "You did an exceptional job."

"Thanks. I had a lot of help."

"Nonetheless, Camp I Can is your brainchild. That's an enormous accomplishment."

"I guess we'll see this summer when it all comes together."

"I know I won't be disappointed." He glanced around. "Can I walk you to your car?"

Rebecca had boxed up the last of the cookies, and Chaney had rinsed the coffeemakers. On their way out, the two of them waved goodbye. "I guess so."

Justin looked for the lights and switched off the overhead fluorescents. They stepped into an elevator, and she was reminded of the last time they'd been in an elevator together—at the Lighthouse Inn. He took the bag she was carrying. "Where's Anna tonight?"

"My dad came over to stay with her. He does a pretty good job of baby-sitting."

"What about your mother?"

"She's working at it. We had a heart-to-heart and she decided she'd rather be a part of our lives than not. She's still not running over to check on Anna's every move, but at least she's not denying her existence or hounding me any longer."

"That's progress."

"Very much so."

The elevator came to a stop and they walked across the lobby and out into the brisk night air. "Where are you parked?" he asked.

"That way."

He walked beside her toward the edge of the lot. She used her key chain to unlock the car doors. He opened the back door and placed her bag on the seat.

She moved to open the driver door, but he placed his hand over the handle. Meredith looked up in surprise.

Without another word, he leaned forward and kissed her. His lips were warm and hungry, and the taste of him made her ache with familiar want.

He drew away, looking down at her face in the darkness. Behind him, a security light made a halo around his head and shoulders. She sensed that he was waiting for her reaction.

All she felt was robbed.

Robbed of the joy his kiss gave her, robbed of the sense of warmth and security that came with Justin's arms.

She flung her arms up and around his shoulders to kiss him back. A hundred warning alarms went off in her head, but her heart ignored them.

Eighteen

She couldn't get close enough. She wanted to experience his warmth and the pleasure he gave. She needed to recapture the way he made her feel—beautiful and sensual and complete. In his embrace she became a desirable woman, and she craved the feeling.

Justin framed her face with his strong hands and rained kisses over her cheeks, her eyelids, her nose.

She grasped his wrists and pulled herself up to meet his lips.

"Meredith," he said, his lips against her cheek. "Knowing that you think I betrayed you has been like a weight on my heart. It's killing me."

"I'm sorry." She worked her hands inside his suit

jacket, found the warmth and firmness of skin and muscle beneath his shirt and held him tightly. "You were right about me. I prided myself on being independent, but that was just because I was afraid to trust anyone. I didn't trust myself, either, because I'd made mistakes and second-guessed my own choices."

"Your reactions were justified, considering what you went through before," he told her.

She tried to shake her head, but he held her fast. "You hadn't given me any cause to mistrust you."

"Do you believe me now?"

"Leslie told me that the board set you up. She also told me you let them know you were angry about it."

"I would resign from the Children's Connection altogether if I thought it would make a difference," he assured her. He'd said it before, and both times his willingness to sacrifice had surprised her.

"There's no need for that."

He hugged her close, and his clean, masculine scent triggered a flood of sensual memories.

"I didn't hold out much hope before I met you," he said, his voice a rumble beneath her ear.

"What do you mean?"

"I had a good marriage, you know. I wasn't looking."

"I know." She leaned away to see his face. "It's okay to say that. It's okay that you loved your wife. I'm not threatened. It tells me you're a loving, devoted man with deep feelings."

"I didn't expect to feel this way," he told her. "And I know there'll never be anyone else for me but you."

Meredith's heart hammered in expectation.

"I love you," he said softly.

She closed her eyes to savor the words, and as soon as she did, Justin's lips closed over hers.

She kissed him back, feeling something more deeply personal than she'd ever known. A connection. *Acceptance.* "Come home with me now," she said.

"Are you sure?"

She nodded. "But I don't want to be separated. For the drive I mean."

"I'll drive and we'll come back for your car."

He took her hand and they hurried across the parking lot. They stopped beside a black BMW, where Justin unlocked the passenger door and held it while she got in. The interior smelled unmistakably like leather.

"Nice car," she commented. "I should have figured you didn't drive the other one to work."

"Mauli drives that one when we're not vacationing." He leaned toward her.

She snuggled up against him and he kissed her breathless, until setting her away so he could drive. Her heart fluttering, Meredith found his hand and held it. Sweet anticipation built inside her.

Pulling into her driveway and parking beside her father's car, he asked, "What about your dad?"

"I'm an adult. He stopped interviewing my friends years ago." She got out her lipstick and applied it quickly, then combed her fingers through her hair.

"Okay." He got out, crossed to her door and escorted her to the house.

Meredith's fingers trembled slightly as she unlocked the door and led him inside.

Her father was seated comfortably in her small family room, watching *The Practice*. Seeing Justin, he used the remote to turn off the TV and stood.

"Dad, this is Justin Weber," she said. "He's volunteered to handle the legal work for the camp. Justin, this is my dad, Hank Malone."

"How do you do, sir?" Justin said, stepping forward to shake his hand.

"Good," her father replied, his expression surprised, but not shocked at Justin's presence. "She was perfect," he said to Meredith. "She had the bottle about two hours ago and has been sleeping in her crib since. I've checked on her at least ten times."

She smiled. "She sleeps longer when she gets a bottle than when she has breast milk."

Her dad looked a little flustered at that comment. "Well, I'll be heading out. Thanks for letting me come take care of her."

Meredith laughed. "I'm supposed to thank you for doing it."

"Oh, okay."

"Thanks, Dad."

"You're welcome. Call me tomorrow." He picked up a glass and plate and carried them to the kitchen, then got his jacket. "Nice to meet you," he said, regarding Justin with a serious look.

"You, too, sir."

Meredith walked him out to his car.

"Is he really just a volunteer?" he asked perceptively. "Or is he something more?"

She was relieved to tell him the truth. "He's definitely something more, Dad."

"Someone permanent?"

"I don't know."

She knew the silence that followed was their mutual contemplation of her mother. "We'll deal with it when we come to it," she said.

He nodded.

She gave her father a hug and watched him drive off.

Inside, she turned the bolt lock and switched off the porch light.

Justin was standing in the kitchen doorway, his suit jacket over his arm.

Taking it from him, she draped it over the back of a dining chair. She then proceeded to loosen his tie, pausing to kiss him when she had it off.

"What do you think he thought?" Justin asked. "Did he say anything outside?"

"I don't know, and yes, he asked if you were

something more than a volunteer." She worked on his shirt buttons until they were unfastened, then tugged his shirttail from his pants. He helped her take it off.

"What did you say?"

"I said yes." She placed his shirt and tie on the oak table and glanced at his shoes.

He knelt to untie them and then slipped them off. "Are you trying to get me naked?"

"I've missed you" was her reply. She had him raise his arms so she could pull his white undershirt over his head. His smooth, dark skin was warm against her lips as she pressed kisses up his belly to his chest.

He eyed her trim black suit and heels. "It's getting a little one-sided."

"Uh-huh." She pointed to his socks, which he stripped off. She unfastened his belt and suit pants and, after he stepped out of them, draped them neatly over another chair. He stood in a pair of tight gray boxer briefs, his growing arousal apparent. "Want to see my bedroom?"

One side of his sexy mouth turned up in a smile. "Sure."

Meredith took his hand and led him through the house, pausing to check on Anna sleeping soundly in the nursery, then into her room. She switched on a tiny lamp with a beaded fringe shade and it lent an amber glow to the elegant space.

Her bedroom was one of her few extravagances,

holding an enormous sleigh bed with a down comforter, satin sheets and mounds of pillows, all in shades of ivory and burnt sienna.

Meredith flung back the covers and urged Justin to the edge of her bed, where he sat and pulled her between the V of his thighs.

From her position above, she bent to kiss him. He slid one hand up the back of her leg, beneath her skirt and caressed her bottom.

She leisurely removed her jacket and laid it at the end of the bed.

He unfastened a few buttons and nudged his nose into the opening of her white blouse where he could nuzzle the swell of her breasts above her lacy bra. "You smell incredible," he said on a groan. "After our week together, I've thought about you every time I smelled coffee."

She laughed delightedly and gave herself over to the sensations his lips were creating on her skin. Her blouse drifted to the floor and she reached back to unfasten her bra. Watching his reaction, she let the garment fall away.

Justin cupped her full breasts reverently. With gentle fingertips, he traced the scars she'd been so self-conscious about and pulled her forward so he could kiss her there.

"I think you're beautiful all over," he told her with gruff emotion in his voice.

In moments her panty hose and skirt were gone, along with his boxers, and the two of them stretched out together on the cool, luxurious sheets. Justin worshipped her body with his hands and lips, whispered words of praise and adoration, and told her again that he loved her.

She laid her hand along his jaw and looked into his eyes in the semidarkness. "I never knew I could feel this way about someone," she told him, her heart in her voice. "I was miserable without you. Even though we'd only known each other for a short time, I felt as though we were meant to be together."

"I guess we can thank the board of Children's Connection, instead of being angry with them," he answered.

"Maybe we should send them flowers," she teased.

"Maybe we should invite them to our wedding," he countered.

Her heart skipped a beat, and she couldn't speak.

"Will you marry me, Meredith?"

Emotion welled inside her and tears blurred her vision. "I love you," she said, her voice trembling.

He hugged her soundly and rolled her to her back, easing his weight upon her. "Was that a yes?"

She nodded. "A definite yes."

Their lips met in a sweet demonstration of the devotion they had just declared. Where before their passion had always run hot and urgent, it now took a tender, more adoring direction, as though they had their whole lives to experience each other, and this was only the beginning.

"I love you," he whispered as he entered her body, making her sigh with the exquisite pleasure.

"I love you," she said when the rhythm grew more demanding and he held her arms above her head.

"I love you," he assured her, sensing her readiness, taking her over the edge and quickly following.

"I love you," she sighed, holding him close and feeling the beat of his heart against hers.

"I have to go," he said two hours later. He lay stretched across her bed, his dark limbs tangled in her shiny sheets.

"I don't want you to leave."

A cry sounded from the other room.

Justin pushed up. "Let me go get her." A few minutes later, he carried Anna in from her crib. Meredith had moved to the cozy chair beside her bed. "I remembered how to do the diaper thing," he said.

As always the sight of her baby in his arms moved her. He handed Anna to her and watched her place the baby at her breast.

His mouth curved up in a tender smile. He sat at her feet and leaned against her leg, where he could reach Anna's head and caress it. "Meredith, let's not wait."

She met his eyes, which were filled with tenderness.

"I want to be with you," he said.

She wanted the same. "Do you want to announce it right away?"

"I want to give you a ring first," he said. "And then we can tell everyone."

"Okay."

"Will you have dinner with me tomorrow evening?"

She didn't even have to think about it. "Yes."

He got up, found his underwear and pulled them on. As though sensing her gaze, he paused.

She admired his form, remembering undressing him in her dining room.

"What?" he said.

"Just looking."

"Do you want to help me pick out the ring today, or do you want to be surprised? I don't mind, either way."

"I trust you."

He stopped, obviously absorbing the enormous impact of that statement. "Okay. Good." He glanced around.

"Your clothes are downstairs."

"I hate to ask, but do you want to get your car tonight?"

She glanced at Anna, thinking she didn't want to take her out so late.

"Why don't I come by in the morning and pick you up? I'll give you a ride to work and that way you won't have to go out."

"That would be great. As long as it doesn't throw off your schedule."

"I'll make it my schedule. Be right back."

Several minutes later, he returned dressed, his jacket and tie over his arm. He was so handsome, he took her breath away. She looked from him to the baby at her breast. Her heart swelled with love for both the man and the child with which she'd been blessed.

Justin knelt beside her chair. He touched Anna's hair, then leaned in to kiss Meredith. "Soon," he promised. "We'll be together soon."

She leaned her head against the hand he raised to touch her cheek. "Do you think you can learn to love my baby?" she asked.

"I already do. She's part of you."

"Do you think Lamond and Jonah will accept me? I won't try to replace their mother. I've always wanted a family, Justin. I'll love your sons and take care of them as if they were my own."

His dark eyes took on a sheen in the lamplight. "We'll work through it," he assured her. "They've asked about you and Anna, and they'll be delighted that you're going to be a permanent part of our lives."

"Justin," she said, "you should be aware that my mother will…be a problem."

"Warning noted."

"No, I mean a *problem*. Her biggest issue with Anna was that her friends might think I slept with a black man to conceive her. I don't know how she'll react once she knows I really *am* sleeping with a black man."

"Meredith, you won a battle with cancer, survived a bad relationship, had a child on your own and raised a half-million dollars for your kids. Have you lost your audacity when it comes to an interracial marriage?"

She laughed. "I'm as audacious as ever—more so if you're by my side."

"I always will be."

"Do you always have the right words?"

"I can be very persuasive," he told her.

"And thorough," she said with a smile, remembering one of their first conversations.

"Don't forget charming," he added.

She smiled then and turned to kiss his palm. "I haven't forgotten for a moment." For the first time a thought occurred to her and she stared at him.

"What?" he asked.

"What about *your* parents? What will they think of you wanting to marry me? Wait, what about your in-laws—the boys' grandparents?"

He placed a kiss on her nose. "They'll all think I have incredible taste in women."

Meredith sat in her parents' kitchen a few days later, the infant seat atop the island. Her mother bustled about preparing tea and setting out a coffee cake.

"Did Dad tell you I was seeing someone?" Meredith asked.

"He mentioned it."

"Did he tell you anything specific about him?"

"He said he was a lawyer and that he's volunteering his services for the camp. Meredith," she said, straightening and wiping her hands on a dish towel, "I don't know what I can do, but I want to volunteer, too. Can you use me somewhere?"

Caught off guard, Meredith gathered her thoughts. "Well, sure. There are plenty of things to be done."

"Very well, then," Veronica said, "that's settled." She ventured a glance at Anna who had begun to fuss.

Meredith got up and dug through the diaper bag for the thermometer. "I'm worried she's coming down with something. She's had a touch of diarrhea and she's been so cranky. It's not like her."

Veronica placed the backs of her fingers against Anna's cheek, then felt her head. "Is she cutting teeth?"

Meredith blinked. "I don't know. How can you tell?"

Her mother rubbed her index finger across Anna's upper and lower gums and Anna bit down on her finger.

"My doctor said teething doesn't cause a fever," Meredith said.

"What a bunch of rubbish. Ask any mother and she'll disagree."

"Really?"

"Her gum is swollen right here. And see how it looks sort of white?" Veronica showed Meredith the spot on Anna's gum.

"That's a tooth?"

"I'd bet a dime to a dollar. Stop on your way home and buy some of that stuff that makes it numb."

Meredith smiled. "Her first tooth!" Her expression quickly dimmed. "It stinks that it has to hurt."

Veronica agreed and poured the tea.

"You know, that's the first time you've acted like a grandmother," Meredith told her.

Slicing the cake, Veronica shrugged.

Uneasy about how her mother would accept what she was going to tell her, Meredith girded herself for battle. "We need to talk."

Her mother laid down the knife and folded her hands as though she'd been anticipating something.

"Sit down," Meredith said.

The woman sat on a kitchen chair and directed her suspicious gaze to her daughter.

"I'm going to get married," she blurted.

Her mother's eyes widened with surprise. "Has Sean come back?"

"No! Hell, no. Sean is out of the picture. I'm marrying Justin Weber. I met him on my vacation and we fell in love. It's real. It's permanent. He was married once before and has two sons. We'll be a blended family."

Her mother seemed to be absorbing the news. "He is a lawyer," she said approvingly.

"Yes, he is."

"But two children. Are you prepared to take on that responsibility?"

"Yes, they're adorable little boys. And he'll be accepting my child as his own, too."

Her mother's eyebrows rose with concern. "Meredith," she said, "it doesn't bother him that…that Anna is…"

"Half African-American?" Meredith finished for her.

"Yes, that."

Meredith's heart fluttered anxiously. She pursed her lips and drew a breath, drawing courage. "It's a non-issue for him."

Veronica absorbed her reply with a nod of her head. "Well," she said, as though groping for something positive to say, "that's a plus for him."

Meredith strapped on her emotional armor and plunged forward. "Justin is an African-American."

Her mother blinked.

The clock on the kitchen wall ticked loudly.

Anna made a little gurgling noise.

Meredith thought she might throw up, waiting for

her mother's reaction. A minute passed where she wondered if the woman had heard her.

Veronica's gaze bored into hers. Finally she said, "Your mind is made up?"

"Yes. I love him. He makes me happy and he accepts me and my baby. I want him in my life forever."

Tears formed in her mother's eyes and she blinked them back. "I fought you over Anna and I didn't win," she said. "In fact I almost lost you."

Meredith's hopes were raised.

"I'm not going to say I agree with this decision. I can't even say right now that I'll ever be happy about it. But I won't criticize you or fight it."

"Thank you."

"He *is* a lawyer," she said, finding something she could appreciate.

"An extremely successful lawyer," Meredith added. "But he's more. He's a warm, generous, kind man. A good father and a loving partner. You're going to like him."

Veronica took a breath and flattened her palms on the table. "How long do I have to get used to the idea?"

"We're going to announce our engagement tomorrow."

Meredith was encouraged. Her mother had shown more poise than she'd imagined, and Meredith couldn't wait to tell Justin and to arrange for their families to meet.

They might still have a few obstacles to overcome, but she had every confidence that their love was bigger than anything they would come up against. She'd never backed away from a challenge before, and love was no exception.

Epilogue

Guests streamed into the Tanglewood Country Club on the evening of Justin and Meredith's reception. Terrence and Leslie Logan had insisted upon throwing the party in honor of their engagement.

"You deserve a party," Leslie declared, standing with her slender hand on her husband's black sleeve. "After the manipulative way the board set you up to meet, it's the least we can do."

"I've assured you there are no hard feelings," Meredith told her. "In a way, the board did us a favor."

"But don't tell them that," Justin added. "Meredith just might have a lifetime benefactor in Wayne

Thorpe. Writing checks to the camp appears to ease his guilt."

Meredith cast him a playful scowl.

"And you've set a date?" Terrence asked, changing the subject.

"We have," Justin answered. "But we're keeping it a secret for now."

"Why is that, dears?" Leslie asked.

"So we can elope without anyone knowing," Justin replied.

Leslie looked surprised. "No big wedding?"

Meredith leaned into Justin's side and he wrapped his arm around her. "We don't want to wait," she said and blushed.

Justin grinned and kissed the top of her head.

"Isn't young love grand?" Leslie turned her unique brown gaze from Meredith to her husband.

His warm look and the hand he placed over hers implied that mature love wasn't so bad, either.

"You two enjoy yourselves now," Leslie said, and the couple moved off into the crowd.

Justin left Meredith's side for a few minutes and returned with drinks. "Yours is club soda and lime," he said.

She had been admiring the elegantly appointed room's rich wood paneling, high ceiling and gilt-framed paintings. "Do you belong to this country club?"

Justin nodded.

"Goodness, Justin, just how much money do you make?"

He gave her a yearly figure and she choked on her club soda.

As he patted her on the back, he added, "But I don't pay for the membership out of pocket. It's one of the job perks."

"Like the suites?"

"The same."

She studied his face. "You make that kind of money, own a Lexus for the family and drive a BMW to work. You have a great home, a live-in nanny…" She paused. "A housekeeper?"

He confirmed her question with a nod.

"But you would have given up all that if I'd asked you?"

"I could work anywhere," he answered.

Mauli came up beside them and gave Meredith a brief hug. "I'm so happy for the two of you. You didn't have me fooled for a minute. I knew you were meant for each other."

Meredith made a comical face. "You had more confidence than I did, then."

Mauli smiled. "Justin assured me my job is mine for as long as I like. Will helping with Anna be part of my duties?"

"Only if you want her to be part of your duties," Meredith said.

The nanny looked delighted. "I do." She glanced behind Meredith. "There she is."

Holding Anna, Meredith's father approached. The baby, dressed in a frilly red dress with white lace trim, white anklets and tiny black patent shoes, was snuggled in the crook of his arm. She took in her surroundings with wide-eyed wonder and smiled her precious one-tooth smile at her mother.

"May I hold her for a while?" Mauli asked.

Hank reluctantly turned his granddaughter over to the nanny, then asked, "Where are your boys, Justin?"

"We arranged to have game tables set up along the east wall over there." Justin pointed. "Last time I looked, there were several kids playing with them."

Mauli excused herself and carried the baby off into the gathering just as Veronica joined them.

Hank put his arm around his wife and said to Justin, "This country club is impressive."

"Do you golf?" Justin asked.

"Occasionally."

"There's a championship course." The two men talked golf for a few minutes and Justin invited Hank to join him the following week. "There's a tennis court," Justin said to Veronica.

"I've never played tennis," she replied uncomfortably.

"The outdoor pool won't be open for a few

months, but there's an indoor pool. And a complete exercise facility with trainers. Maybe you and Meredith would enjoy an afternoon together."

"Maybe." She didn't sound excited about the idea.

"The food in the dining room is excellent," he suggested, still trying to find something to catch her interest.

Veronica managed to look Justin in the eye and gave him a weak smile. She hadn't been easily won over, but during their recent encounters Justin had proven his ability to persuade and charm. He would probably never be her first choice for her daughter's husband, but Veronica had grudgingly accepted that Meredith loved him and would not change her mind.

"I could reserve a table for you and your friends some afternoon," Justin suggested. "My treat."

Veronica's eyebrows raised with interest. "That would be lovely."

Holding back a giggle, Meredith found Justin's hand and squeezed it. He smiled down and leaned to give her a quick kiss.

Sometime later, several of the camp volunteers surrounded them with good wishes and a flurry of hugs. The engaged couple had offered a blanket invitation to the party to anyone involved in Camp I Can, and many of them had shown up.

Justin and Meredith continued to be surprised at the number of acquaintances they had in common. With Meredith working at Portland General Hospital and Justin at Children's Connection, they were bound to have mutual associates.

Leslie introduced Meredith to Trent Crosby, with whom it turned out Justin was already acquainted. "We diverted a potential problem together recently," Justin told Meredith.

"Where is your sister?" Meredith asked. "Katie promised to help with the camp."

"My sister's spending some time at the family ranch in Wyoming," Trent said.

Before Meredith could voice another question, Trent had excused himself and moved into the crowd.

Rebecca Holley shared plans for a special fund-raising event with all proceeds going to Camp I Can. "I see a lot of problems and unhappiness in my work," she shared openly with them. "But there are miracles, too, and sometimes they need to be initiated by us humans."

Meredith smiled. "I couldn't have found a better fund-raising chair. Thanks."

"Hey, I found *you*," Rebecca teased good-naturedly.

Nancy Allen introduced her guest, Everett Baker, a tall dark-haired man who seemed uncomfortable with his surroundings and the throng of guests.

"Everett works for Children's Connection," Nancy said.

As the clinic's accountant, he and Justin knew each other.

"Accountant?" Meredith asked. "I could use

someone good with numbers to help balance the books and create a budget."

Everett cast her a shy glance. "I'd be glad to help, Miss Malone," he offered.

"Don't mind her," Justin said. "She'd recruit her own mother for the cause."

Meredith laughed. "Didn't have to. She volunteered."

Everett's smile didn't reach his brown eyes. There was something naggingly familiar about the man, but Meredith couldn't put her finger on what it was.

They were joined by another handsome man with dark hair and eyes.

"Meredith, this is Peter Logan. Peter, my soon-to-be wife, Meredith, Nancy Allen and Everett Baker."

Peter shook hands with each person to whom he'd been introduced.

"I'm assuming you're one of 'the' Logans," Meredith said in a friendly tone.

"Terrence and Leslie's oldest," he replied easily.

"Peter is now CEO of Logan Corporation," Justin told her. "As of, what, about two years now?"

Peter nodded. "Struggling to fill some big shoes."

Justin slapped him on the shoulder in one of those classically masculine gestures. "As if a Harvard business grad doesn't have the feet to fill them."

Everett leaned over and quietly said something to Nancy, who interrupted to make their goodbyes.

"Congratulations once again on your engagement," she told the happy couple. "We're going to go freshen our drinks." She and Everett moved away.

Chaney arrived sometime later, late as usual, and attired in a wild zebra-print dress, her hair a new shade of red that was shocking, even for Chaney.

She carried a small gift box and presented it to the newly engaged couple.

"Go ahead, open it," she said to Justin.

He untied the ribbon and lifted the lid. A pair of matching gold watches lay on a bed of black velvet, one men's, one women's. "Understated and elegant, right?" Chaney asked, her gold hoop earrings swaying.

"Chaney, they're incredible." Meredith lifted the smaller one from the box.

"Probably not as nice as your last one," she said to Justin, "but I knew yours was pretty much toast."

He glanced from Chaney to Meredith. "This was really nice of you," he said, leaning over to hug Chaney. "Thank you."

"You're welcome." Accepting a glass of wine from a tray a passing waiter carried, she took a sip and glanced around. "Classy place. You're marrying well, Mer."

Meredith grinned. She was well aware of how fortunate she was to have found the man of her heart's desire, and the fact that he was handsome and well-off was just the frosting on the proverbial cake. "I know."

Chaney turned her full attention to Justin. "So you don't have a brother?"

He shook his head. "No, I don't."

"Is your father married?"

Meredith groaned.

"To my *mother*," Justin said with a smile.

"Yeah." Not discouraged, Chaney went on. "Do you have any single friends? I prefer at least an eight, but a five would do."

Justin's perplexed expression had Meredith chuckling.

The band struck up a tune, and he took her hand. "If you'll excuse us," he said to Chaney, "we're going to have our first dance."

The crowd parted and a smattering of applause followed them.

As Justin took her in his arms and led her smoothly across the floor, Meredith's heart swelled with a newly born sense of love and acceptance.

The most wonderful man in the world loved her.

She had a beautiful baby and a new family, not to mention friends and co-workers who supported her dreams.

What more could a girl want?

* * * * *

*Turn the page for a sneak preview
of the emotional* LOGAN'S LEGACY *title,*
INTIMATE SURRENDER
*by popular author RaeAnne Thayne
on sale in January 2005...*

Katie Crosby had just added another log to the fire in the massive river-rock fireplace of the great room and was settling onto the comfy couch with a mug of hot cocoa and a book she knew she wouldn't be able to concentrate on when she heard the bass rumble of a vehicle approaching.

What had Margie and Clint forgotten? she wondered. At this rate, they would find themselves stuck out here in the middle of the approaching blizzard.

A blast of cold air hit her as soon as she hurried to open the door for them. She shivered and saw that in the short time since she had stood in the driveway watching them leave, a half inch of snow had fallen.

The sun had slid behind the mountains and in the pale lavender twilight, she could make out a late-model SUV approaching the house.

Not Clint and Margie, then. Odd. They hadn't mentioned they were expecting anyone.

From the entryway, she watched a man climb out of the vehicle and had an impression of lean, muscular strength. She saw only dark wavy hair and a leather aviator jacket, then he turned to face her and the stoneware mug slipped from her stupid, clumsy fingers.

She reached for it just in time to keep the whole thing from gushing out all over the wood floor. Hot cocoa splashed her jeans but she barely registered it. She could focus on only one horrifying realization.

He had found her!

She couldn't seem to draw enough breath into her lungs as Peter Logan slammed the SUV door shut and stalked up the porch stairs. The blood rushed away from her oxygen-starved brain and she swayed, fighting a panicked urge to slam the door and shove the heavy hall table across it as a barricade against his anger. It took every ounce of concentration to keep her hands clenched tightly at her sides, not covering the tiny, barely there life growing inside her.

"Hello, Celeste." Her middle name came out more like a snarl.

"Peter. Th-this is a surprise." She hated the stammer but couldn't seem to help it.

"I'll just bet it is."

She couldn't think what to say, could only stare at him as wild memories crowded through her mind of how that tight, angry mouth had once been tender and sensual, had once explored every inch of her skin.

"Are you going to stand there staring at me all night like I'm the Abominable Snowman come to call, or do you think you might condescend to let me inside?"

Did she have a choice? If she did, her vote would have been for locking him out in the porch rather than face a confrontation with him. But since she had a pretty good idea that a man like Peter Logan wouldn't let anything as inconsequential as a locked door keep him away, she had no choice but to surrender to the inevitable. She stepped aside.

"What are you doing here, Peter?"

"You mean how did I figure out who the hell you really were?"

Despite her best efforts at control, she shivered at the menace in his tone. "That, too."

"Don't you read the papers, sweetheart?"

She stared at him blankly. Across the vast room, she was oddly aware of a log breaking apart in the fireplace with a hiss and crackle. After a moment he yanked a folded newspaper from the inside pocket of his snow-flecked leather jacket and slapped it down on the narrow hall table next to her.

She eyed it like he'd just let loose a wolverine in the Sweetwater great room. Warily, her pulse skipping with sudden trepidation, Katie picked up the newspaper. It was a copy of the society page of *Portland Weekly,* the independent tabloid that delighted in poking fun at the city's movers and shakers.

Her gaze went to the photo first and her already queasy stomach dipped. It was a photo of her and the man now standing before her, both of them in elegant evening wear. Her back—bared in a glittery designer gown she'd borrowed from her best friend—was to the camera, but anybody who saw the picture could clearly identify Peter Logan— and could see the two of them were locked in a passionate embrace.

She had seen it before—the newspaper had run the photo in December as part of a feature spread of a bachelor auction and charity benefit for a Portland fertility clinic. The caption had said only something about Peter being photographed in a hot kiss with a mystery woman. When they ran it the first time, she had seen it and thanked her very lucky stars that she hadn't been recognizable.

Apparently someone had figured it out. The headline above the photo read Mystery Solved: Crosby

And Logan Scions Put Aside Famous Feud Long Enough For Kiss.

Oh no. She drew in a shaky breath. This was bad. Seriously bad. She read on.

We first brought you the juicy tidbit a few months ago that Logan Corporation CEO and oh-so-sexy bachelor Peter Logan was caught in a very heated embrace with a mysterious glamour-gal during a chichi gala for the Children's Connection clinic, a cause the Logan family notably supports. The two of them disappeared together soon after.

At the time, Logan pointedly refused to answer questions about the object of his affection, but after some digging *Portland Weekly* has since learned his snuggle-honey was none other than Katherine Crosby. That's right, of *those* Crosbys. The Logans' rivals on and off the corporate battlefield.

Does their embrace signal an end to the famous feud? Are Portland's own versions of the Hatfield and McCoy clans really ready to kiss and make up?

Apparently at least two of them are.

Neither Logan nor Ms. Crosby were available for comment, but we'll bring you more about this exciting development as soon as we learn anything.

Her already queasy stomach dipped. Sheila was bound to hear about this, Katie had no doubt whatsoever about that. And when she did, Katie knew her mother would rage and carry on for days, accusing her of everything from disloyalty to outright treason.

Just thinking about the inevitable scene made her shoulders sag with the exhaustion that never seemed far away these days.

"Nothing to say?" Peter finally asked when her silence dragged on.

"I've never been called a glamour-gal before. I don't believe it's as gratifying as I would have imagined."

His sculpted features darkened. "I dislike being made a fool of, Katherine."

"Kate," she murmured, regretting the glibness she tended to turn to during times of high stress. "Nearly everyone calls me Katie or Kate."

"Really, Celeste?" he asked in that same biting tone.

Oh, Katie. What a mess you're in. Pregnant with this man's baby, this overwhelming, powerful, *gorgeous* man who despised her and her family. If he hated her now, how would he react if he ever discovered the tiny secret she carried inside her?

The fragile threads of control seemed to slip a few more notches but she flailed for them valiantly and faced him with what she hoped was cool aplomb.

Without waiting for the invitation she wasn't sure she could issue, he yanked off his jacket and tossed it over the rack of entwined elk antlers in the hallway then claimed one of the plump armchairs near the fire. Kate really had no choice but to follow him. She perched on the edge of the sofa, trying not to let him see her nervousness.

"Okay, let's hear it. What's your game?"

"Game?"

"What are you playing at? What were you trying to achieve by your little masquerade?"

Of course he would want explanations from her, some justification for her deception. How could she possibly find the words for something she didn't even understand herself?

"Why didn't you tell me who you were?"

"I don't know that I have a good answer to that."

"Try." His voice was silk-sheathed steel.

She scrambled for some kind of explanation and finally came up with something she hoped sounded reasonable. It was part of the truth, just not all of it. "Katie Crosby is a fairly boring person," she said after a long moment. "All she ever thinks about is work. I suppose it was exciting being someone else for a few hours. Someone glamorous and adventurous and…and desirable. I got carried away by the magic of the evening. Then, after we…we kissed, I was afraid to tell you who I was. I knew you would be angry and it just seemed easier all around not to say anything."

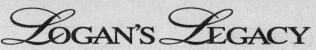

LOGAN'S LEGACY

Because birthright has its privileges and family ties run deep.

Silhouette Books invites you to come back and visit the Logan family!

Just collect six (6) proofs of purchase from the back of six (6) different LOGAN'S LEGACY titles and receive FOUR free LOGAN'S LEGACY books that are not not currently available in retail outlets!

Just complete the order form and send it, along with six (6) proofs of purchase from six (6) different LOGAN'S LEGACY titles to: LOGAN'S LEGACY, P.O. Box 9047, Buffalo, NY 14269-9047, or P.O. Box 613, Fort Erie, Ontario L2A 5X3. (No cost for shipping and handling)

Name (PLEASE PRINT)

Address _____ Apt. #

City _____ State/Prov. _____ Zip/Postal Code

093 KJY DXH6

When you return six proofs of purchase, you will receive the following titles:

**THE GREATEST RISK by Cara Colter
WHAT A MAN NEEDS by Patricia Thayer
UNDERCOVER PASSION by Raye Morgan
ROYAL SEDUCTION by Donna Clayton**

Remember—to receive all four (4) titles, you must send six (6) original proofs of purchase. (Please allow 4-8 weeks for delivery. Offer expires August 31, 2005. Offer available in Canada and the U.S. only.)

When you respond to this offer, we will also send you *Inside Romance*, a free quarterly publication, highlighting upcoming releases and promotions from Harlequin and Silhouette Books.

❑ If you do not wish to receive this free publication, please check here.

Silhouette®
Where love comes alive™

LOGAN'S LEGACY

Because birthright has its privileges and family ties run deep.

ONE PROOF OF PURCHASE
LLPOP7

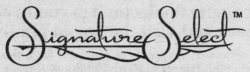
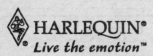

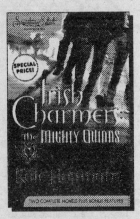
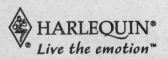

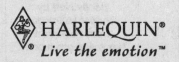